Something _____ and he nearly lost his balance. He thought he was going to be sick. That would serve them right. He would puke all over them, whoever they were.

They? As in more than one?

Up? When the hell had he fallen down?

He was going to beat the shit out of them too. Just as soon as he got up again.

He felt another hard knock on the back of his head. He was lying facedown now, although again he did not recall just how he got there. He could feel rough hands pulling at him. Rolling him onto his back.

The gun. His Colt. Where was it?

He tried to draw the revolver, but his hand was not co-operating very well. It refused to do what he was telling it.

Longarm tried to cuss the sons of bitches, but the best he could manage was a faint exhalation of what precious little breath he had left.

"You! Get away from that man."

The voice was loud. And shrill. And female.

Longarm heard the crunch of feet on gravel and then pounding footsteps as his assailants fled.

That was the last thing he remembered . . .

TABOR EVANS

LONGARM

AND THE SABOTAGED RAILROAD

J

JOVE BOOKS, NEW YORK

THE BERKLEY PUBLISHING GROUP
Published by the Penguin Group
Penguin Group (USA) Inc.
375 Hudson Street, New York, New York 10014, USA
Penguin Group (Canada), 90 Eglinton Avenue East, Suite 700, Toronto, Ontario M4P 2Y3, Canada
(a division of Pearson Penguin Canada Inc.)
Penguin Books Ltd., 80 Strand, London WC2R 0RL, England
Penguin Group Ireland, 25 St. Stephen's Green, Dublin 2, Ireland (a division of Penguin Books Ltd.)
Penguin Group (Australia), 250 Camberwell Road, Camberwell, Victoria 3124, Australia
(a division of Pearson Australia Group Pty. Ltd.)
Penguin Books India Pvt. Ltd., 11 Community Centre, Panchsheel Park, New Delhi—110 017, India
Penguin Group (NZ), Cnr. Airborne and Rosedale Roads, Albany, Auckland 1310, New Zealand
(a division of Pearson New Zealand Ltd.)
Penguin Books (South Africa) (Pty.) Ltd., 24 Sturdee Avenue, Rosebank, Johannesburg 2196,
South Africa

Penguin Books Ltd., Registered Offices: 80 Strand, London WC2R 0RL, England

LONGARM AND THE SABOTAGED RAILROAD

A Jove Book / published by arrangement with the author

PRINTING HISTORY
Jove edition / January 2007

Copyright © 2007 by The Berkley Publishing Group.

ISBN: 978-0-515-14243-3

JOVE®
Jove Books are published by The Berkley Publishing Group,
a division of Penguin Group (USA) Inc.,
375 Hudson Street, New York, New York 10014.
JOVE is a registered trademark of Penguin Group (USA) Inc.
The "J" design is a trademark belonging to Penguin Group (USA) Inc.

PRINTED IN THE UNITED STATES OF AMERICA

10 9 8 7 6 5 4 3 2 1

Chapter 1

"Mornin', ma'am."

"Good morning to you, sir."

"May I say that you look mighty fetchin' for it bein' so early in the day? Uh-huh. Mighty fine-looking filly, you are."

"You are very forward, sir."

"And you, Miss Fancy Britches, might could make me swallow that except for the fact that your left tit is peekin' out from under that sheet," Longarm said with a grin.

Caroline laughed and swept the sheet away, exposing considerably more than that one breast. The only thing she was "wearing" was a patch of thick, curly pubic hair. Apart from that dark and silky bush, she was as bare as a boiled egg.

Longarm was just as naked as she was, the difference being that while Caroline was soft, Deputy United States Marshal Custis Long was hard. Or anyway, selected parts of him were.

Longarm bent down and kissed her. Caroline's arms

snaked around his neck and tugged him down on top of her lean and nicely formed body.

"Hey," he protested, wriggling free from her embrace. "Lemme go. I got t' take a leak."

"You have a hard-on. You can't pee with it standing up like that, can you?"

"Oh, it's all right. Just means I might hit the ceiling."

She looked like she believed every word, so he reconsidered the impression that would leave and said, "It'll soften up some as soon as I turn around t' where I can't see you."

"Is that a compliment, kind sir?" she asked, laughing.

"Damn right it is. You are one good-looking an' sexy lady."

"You are not so bad yourself, sir." The words were spoken lightly, but they were also the truth. Women seemed attracted to him, although damned if he could ever understand that fact. Longarm did not consider himself to be much of a catch. But he did not complain that women did.

He was tall, that was true enough, standing over six feet in height. But he did not have the chiseled good looks that could be seen in an illustrated advertisement for men's shirts. Longarm was more rough and craggy than smoothly chiseled.

He had dark brown hair and golden brown eyes that were as warm as melted butter, but could turn instantly to ice if offense were taken.

He had broad, muscular shoulders, a flat belly, and lean hips.

He also had a red, pulsing tent pole poking out of his midsection at the moment.

"Let go, dammit. My bladder's about t' bust."

"Oh . . . all right." Caroline released him, but watched with considerable interest while he knelt to fetch the thunder mug from beneath the bed, the muscles in his back rippling when he moved.

By the time he stood up again, his erection had subsided at least a little so he could release his urine.

Caroline's mane of long, curly hair fell over her shoulders and swung forward to hide her face when she leaned toward him. Unexpectedly, the woman reached out and put her hand into the stream of urine warm from his body, turning her fingers, opening and closing her hand as if washing with Longarm's piss.

"What the hell are you doin', girl?" He finished and reached for a hand towel to wipe himself dry before returning to the bed.

"Don't," she said.

"Don't what?"

"Don't dry off. I want to suck you."

"Fine, but I ain't . . ."

"I know you haven't. Now don't argue with me. Just come over to me. Please."

He turned and took a step forward. Caroline lifted his cock on her wet palm as if weighing it there, then bent her head to him and took him into her mouth. Longarm's erection immediately returned, filling Caroline's mouth as she held his shaft with one wet hand and fondled his balls with her dry one.

After a moment, she lifted her face and smiled up at him. "You taste salty."

"Look, I can wash. It'd only take a minute."

"That was not my point, dear. I like the taste of you. Even that. Would you like to piss in my mouth?"

3

"No, thanks. I can think o' better places to put that."

"Really!" She laughed softly. "Then give me just a few moments more. I am enjoying this." She took him into her mouth again, then ran her tongue up and down his shaft.

Longarm's state of arousal grew to near the bursting point and he warned her, "If you want t' feel that thing inside you, you'd best leave off what you're doing an' spread your legs, girl."

"We can do both, can't we? I could drink your first load. Then we could rest a little while and you could . . . how do you Westerners put it . . . you could climb into the saddle for the second go."

"There ain't much I'd like better, pretty girl, but the reason I got outa bed to begin with is that I got t' get dressed and go to work. I *do* work, you know, unlike your rich boyfriends back East."

She giggled. "Is there anybody you have to shoot today, dear? Can I watch?"

"Lordy, what you don't know about the business of lawing," he moaned. "I don't go off shootin' people all day. I never do it unless it's forced on me."

"Is that part of the code, dear?"

"Code? You been reading too many dime romances. There ain't no code. There's just cold laws and common decency, and me an' fellow badge-toters like me only get involved when somebody breaks those laws. Now are you gonna lay back an' spread yourself open, or d'you want me to just get dressed an' go to work now?"

Caroline answered by playfully—but lightly, thank goodness—nipping the tip of his pecker with her teeth, then lying back on the already rumpled sheets with her legs spread wide for his pleasure.

And pleasure she was too.

Longarm lowered himself onto her, Caroline guiding his entrance with both hands.

He felt the warm, slippery flesh surround him as he eased his way into her body.

Caroline cried out once and shifted her body to more easily accommodate his length. Her arms came up to wrap tight around him, and and a moment later she did the same with her legs, clamping onto Longarm's body as if wanting to hold him there permanently.

Longarm held himself still for a few seconds to give her time to become comfortable with him there; then he began to pump and rotate his hips, slowly at first, and then more rapidly until he was churning deep. Caroline held on, her body meeting his thrusts with her own increasingly wild gyrations until he thought she might tear apart if she did not soon slow down.

He felt the sweet build and surge of pressure in his balls and lower belly and then the sudden outpouring of hot liquid erupting into her. He groaned just a little and plunged deep one last time, holding himself rigid there while his jism flowed.

Longarm felt Caroline tremble and shudder. She cried out, muffling the sound against his shoulder, as her body was ripped with the spasms of her own climax.

He waited for the last warm drops to trickle into her, then let his weight down until he lay limp and loose on the woman's slim body. He marveled anew at the ability of women to so take a man's weight without hurting themselves or impairing their ability to breathe . . . but only in that one timeless position. Marvelous!

"Mmm." Caroline ran her hands gently over his

back, making circles with her fingers and palms. It felt good, much like a massage but light and . . . friendly.

He smiled. "I got t' go, darlin'. I got to go to work."

"Can't I watch you shoot someone?"

"Bloodthirsty wench. No! But I'll tell you what you can watch me shoot."

"Yes?" She sounded eager.

"I'll come back this evening. We'll go t' dinner, you and me, an' then you can watch me shoot this gun here." He moved her hand to his crotch, where his wet cock lay limp and sticky in a nest of short and curlies.

"I can settle for that," Caroline said.

"All right then. It's a promise."

The girl kissed him, but she did not offer any further protest as he stood and moved through her hotel suite, first pouring a little cold water into the washstand basin and using it to hastily sponge himself clean. He dried with a hand towel and made faces in the mirror that sat atop a chest of drawers.

"No time t' shave, dammit," he grumbled, mostly to himself, then reached for his clothing and began to dress.

A few moments later, he stamped his feet into his black stovepipe cavalry boots and strapped on his gun belt, adjusting the position to best facilitate a cross draw from just to the left of his belt buckle. Caroline watched with special fascination as he buckled the gun belt in place.

"Are you sure I can't wat—"

"No, dammit. Besides, I won't be shooting anybody. No shootings on my schedule today. Now go back to sleep. I want you rested and ready to buck t'night."

"Buck? Did you pronounce that correctly, sir?"

Longarm laughed. "That way will do until I get back. Then we'll discuss it."

"Don't forget me."

"Not damn likely." He pulled on his tweed coat and plucked his flat-crowned back Stetson off the hat rack beside the door to her room. Without a backward glance at the still-naked woman, he let himself out and headed for the office.

Chapter 2

U.S. Marshal William Vail's chief clerk, Henry, looked up from the ever-present paperwork on his desk and pursed his lips in disapproval. "You're late."

Longarm's only answer was a grin and a wink. He crossed the room to the coat rack and deposited his Stetson on one of the arms, then sauntered over to one of the wooden armchairs against the wall and took a seat, crossing his legs and reaching for a cheroot as he did so.

"Don't bother to light up. You'll just have to put it out again."

"How the hell come?"

"The boss. He has a cold. He doesn't feel good. And some railroad tycoon was blowing smoke in his face a little while ago. You would have gotten your share of it if you'd been here on time."

"Then I'm double glad that I'm late." Longarm slipped the cheroot back into his coat pocket and uncrossed his legs. "What happened to the he-coon?"

"He had to rush off. Something really important, I'm sure," Henry said, reaching up to adjust the spectacles that rested on the bridge of his nose. They usually looked like they were about to fall off his face, but they never did. Longarm sometimes marveled at Henry's ability to keep them in place,

"Stay there," Henry said. "I'll tell him you finally decided to grace us with your presence."

"It was worth it," Longarm said smugly. Henry had seen her outside the restaurant the evening before. If only he knew . . .

"I'll be right back," Henry said, refusing to rise to the bait.

Henry left his desk, tapped once on the door to Billy Vail's private office, and let himself in without waiting for a response. Henry was only one among the office staff or deputies who was privileged to do that. Anyone else would get his head bitten off if he were so bold. And so stupid.

Henry was back within seconds. He motioned Longarm inside,

"Brace yourself," Henry whispered as Longarm came past. "He isn't very happy right now."

Longarm saw what Henry meant the moment he stepped into Billy's office. The United States marshal appointed to the Department of Justice's Denver District was scowling, his normally pink cheeks and bald head a dark, mottled red, and his eyes were bloodshot and watery. The boss looked like he was steaming.

"I, uh, sorry I'm late." Custis Long rarely apologized. For anything. This time it seemed a pretty good idea.

"You embarrassed me," were Billy's words of greeting. "I had that son of a bitch Hancock sitting in here looking down his patrician nose at me. I made the mistake of telling him you were a good man. Reliable. Then you go and do something like this." Billy leaned back and plucked his watch out of his vest. He snorted and shook his head angrily.

"I been late before this, Boss. That ain't what's graveling you."

Billy lifted his chin and gave Longarm a look that could wither artificial flowers. "Sit down."

"Yes, sir." Longarm sat. And shut his mouth. Maybe he should have turned his back on Caroline this morning when she wanted seconds. Maybe.

Vail deliberately ignored Longarm, concentrating on staring at some papers instead. After a minute or so—it seemed a long time but probably was not—the marshal looked up. "You're right."

"What?" Longarm could not recall what it was he'd said that he might be right about. After all, he'd scarcely uttered a word since he got here. It did not seem prudent, though, to ask Billy for clarification. Not right now.

"It isn't you being late that has me so thoroughly pissed off," Billy said, then quickly added, "although I am not most pleased about that either, you understand."

"Yes, sir," Longarm said, not understanding at all.

"It's just that Bertram Hancock is a pompous asshole. And you being late forced me to suffer his presence longer than should have been necessary."

"Sorry, Boss."

"So you said." Billy frowned, then visibly shuddered and took a moment to peer at his fingernails while he forced personal feelings aside and concentrated on the tasks at hand.

11

"Hancock may be a son of a bitch," Billy said, "but his problem is real."

"And that problem would be . . . ?"

"The man is a major shareholder in the Toynbee and Twin Rocks Railroad. Are you familiar with it?"

Longarm shook his head. "Lord, no. There are so many of those short lines tearing up the mountains it would take a damn accountant to keep track of them all. I don't think I ever heard o' this . . . Toynbee, did you say?"

"Toynbee and Twin Rocks," Billy affirmed. He swung his swivel chair around so that he was facing away from Longarm, pulled an already sodden handkerchief from his pocket, and noisily blew his nose.

"That explains it then. I never heard of either o' them towns neither."

Billy shrugged. "Mining camps, of course. The things sprout up like mushrooms. Then the railroads follow. These camps are over on the west slope."

"They're havin' some sort of trouble, I take it," Longarm said.

The boss nodded. "So far this morning I have received telegram messages from the Attorney General and three United States Congressmen asking me to lend all possible assistance to the Toynbee and Twin Rocks and to Mr. Bertram Hancock of the Pennsylvania Hancocks."

Longarm shrugged. "I don't know none o' them. They ain't on my social calendar."

"More accurate to say that you are not on theirs," Billy said, his voice hoarse and thick.

"Not that I much give a shit," Longarm said, "and I bet they don't neither."

12

"Returning to the point," Billy said firmly, "there seems to be a right-of-way problem with this planned short line."

"And that problem would be?"

"Someone is trying to sabotage the construction."

"Why in the world would they want to involve us in this? Something like that oughta be easy enough to stop, Boss. Just have somebody lay in wait for whoever is doin' whatever, an' the next thing you know the sonuvabitch is either behind bars or laying there dead. Either way the problem is solved."

"Easy for you to say. Not so easy for them to do, I take it. You see, they already know who is behind the sabotage. They just can't catch them at it."

"So they're inept. How does that bring us into it? I don't see no federal law bein' violated here."

"Did I mention the messages I've received today from those Congressmen and the Attorney General? That makes it our business. The justification—as if any were necessary—is that the railroad will receive a contract as a mail carrier. Therefore, any interference with them is de facto interference with the government of the United States of America. Get it?"

"Since you put it that way, Boss . . ."

"I assured Mr. Hancock, the asshole, that my best deputy would be investigating this shocking crime. My best chronically late deputy, I should have said."

"Yes, sir."

"I would appreciate it if you were to avoid embarrassing me further."

"Yes, sir. Point taken. I, uh, believe you said they know who is behind the sabotage?"

"Yes. Apparently the land grant for the rail line was opposed by the Adamson and Sons Express Company. They are a stagecoach line."

"And the current holders o' the mail contract," Longarm guessed. "They don't wanta lose the business an' figure they can keep it as long as there's no railroad reaching into the camps, is that it?"

"Exactly. What I want you to do is to go put a stop to this sabotage so the railroad can build through to Twin Rocks and the mail contracts be let." Billy sniffed. Loudly.

"No problem," Longarm assured him. "No problem at all."

Billy dragged his hanky out and blew his nose again.

Chapter 3

Longarm was what one might call a wee bit casual when it came to the spit and polish of life. When he was not on a case, then he was *really* not on a case, and the hell with picky little details like working hours and paperwork.

That said, he was completely dedicated to the job. He had been known to work seventy-two hours straight through and would back water for neither man nor beast. Well, depending on the beast; he drew the line at going hand-to-hand with bears. The bottom line was that, joking aside, he believed in the sanctity of the law. He believed in what he was doing, and he did it without shirking.

When he walked out of Billy Vail's office, he went to Henry to get a handful of travel vouchers . . . and a clue about where the hell this Toynbee place was, it being the starting point for the Toynbee and Twin Rocks short line.

When he left the office a few minutes later, he started his usual preparations for an assignment. He sent a messenger with a note for Caroline explaining that he had been called out of town. Stopped at a barbershop for a quick shave and a boot-blacking. Checked the time and hailed a hansom cab to take him to his rooming house by way of the Chinese laundry, and minutes later was back in the cab on his way to the Denver, South Park, and Pacific depot.

By this late date, he pretty well had the timetable memorized, at least as to generalities, and knew he still had time to catch a train that would take him across the spine of the Rockies. Once past the first wave of mountains . . . he would just have to figure that out when he got there.

Longarm leaned on the low barrier that separated the stationmaster's desk from the public portion of the room. He had his legs crossed at the ankle, and a slim, dark cheroot was caught between his teeth, its smoke curling up to collect under the brim of his Stetson and pool there for a moment before filtering into the air above him.

"What you are tellin' me," he said in a slow drawl, "is that there ain't no way to get there."

The stationmaster, a man named Jenks, shrugged. "What I am telling you, Marshal, is that of course there is a way to get there. But it is true that there is no *good* way."

"Well, shit," Longarm grumbled.

"If you go all the way to the end of our tracks, you will still have to take a coach back north again through Leadville and on to Gore Creek and meet the road to Glenwood Springs there."

"If you was doing it, Jenks, which way would you take?"

"I'd forget about thinking you could make a comfortable trip of it on our passenger cars. I would take our westbound only as far as Silverthorne and disembark there. At a guess, that would cut a good fifty or sixty miles off the stagecoach leg of your trip." He shrugged again. "Of course, I could be wrong about that. But it is what I would do myself."

"Shit!" Longarm repeated forcefully.

"Do you have any special needs, Marshal? Prisoners? Anything like that?"

Longarm shook his head. "Not goin' out. As for comin' back . . . we shall see." He smiled. "With any kinda luck, I can just go over there an' ruffle up my feathers an' rattle my wings, strut around like a cock lookin' over the hens. They'll all get scared an' vow t' be good boys an' play nice forevermore. Then I can come home an' get back to that little old gal I was sparkin' before sworn duty carried me away from her."

The stationmaster, who was not a handsome man, looked pained. "Bachelors," he mumbled.

Longarm grinned at him. "Nobody made you go an' get married, friend."

"Oh, but that is where you are wrong. Someone did indeed force the issue."

"Her papa?" Longarm said.

Jenks's expression was woeful. He nodded and looked away.

"Could happen to the best of us," Longarm said sympathetically.

The stationmaster looked up and squared his shoulders, obviously forcing his thoughts away from what might have been and back onto the routine matters of the day. "Is there anything else I can do for you, Marshal?"

"No, sir, you done me just fine, thanks."

"Then if you will excuse me . . ." Jenks turned and headed toward his desk with its clutter of schedules, notes, and message forms.

Longarm went in the other direction, out onto the open platform, raw with the stink of smoke and coal dust, gritty underfoot with cinders and dried mud. He liked it a helluva lot better out there on the platform than indoors with only a rolltop desk for a view.

Chapter 4

It was—Longarm tugged the railroad-grade Ingersoll from his vest pocket and checked the time—10:17 at night when he stepped down onto another cinder-gritty, coal-stinking platform, this one on the edge of Silver-thorne. It was dimly lighted with guttering lamps and was cold as the inside of a whore's heart.

Longarm collected his things from the baggage car and, shivering, took them across the platform to an empty hand cart. He set his carpetbag down, unstrapped the lashings and stirrup leathers that held his McClellan saddle in a compact bundle, and set his Winchester and scabbard aside. His sheepskin-lined coat was part of that bundle, and up here at this elevation he damned well needed the extra protection from the breeze and a deep night chill.

Moving quickly and commencing to shiver so hard his teeth chattered, he pulled off the tweed suit coat he customarily wore in the city and exchanged it for the sheepskin. Once he was snugged down inside the soft shearling, he felt considerably better.

19

"Board! All abo-o-o-oard for Breckenridge, Fairplay, and points south. All abo-o-o-oard!"

There were only a few folks still visible on the platform and they quickly disappeared, either into the passenger coaches or drifting away into the town.

Longarm took out a cheroot and "borrowed" flame from one of the oil lamps to light it, then took his time folding and arranging his suit coat so it would not be too badly wrinkled—he hoped. He wrapped it carefully around the rifle scabbard and stowed the whole package of coat, rifle, and leather scabbard inside the padded skirts of the military-style saddle before tidying it all into a heavy, compact bundle.

By the time he was done, the lights on the caboose were completely out of sight and someone inside the station was extinguishing lamps and pulling down shades. A skeleton staff would have to work through the night, the telegraph operator at the very least, and probably an assistant to the stationmaster too, but the office was closed for the night now.

He intended to head into town to see if he could find a room for the remainder of the night. If they were open, he could ask at the stagecoach office about the rest of his trip.

There might be a coach scheduled through during the night and he would take one if he had to, but he would much prefer to get some sleep in a bed than try to catch winks between the bounces and the bumps of a lightly sprung coach on bad roads. He had done that more than enough times before and was not fond of it.

If he could find neither a room nor a coach, however, he could always spend the night bent over a hand of

cards in some smoky, rowdy honky-tonk. He had done
that plenty of times before also, and in a mining town
like Silverthorne the saloons would be open around the
clock to receive miners coming off shift at odd hours of
the day and night.

Longarm picked up the carpetbag in his left hand
and balanced the saddle upside down on his right shoulder, then looked around to decide which direction he
wanted to take, hoping for a hotel or at the very least a
railroaders' boardinghouse.

He heard a flurry of rapid footsteps crunching on
gravel, and then thumping hollowly on the platform as a
young woman wearing only a very light dress dashed
out of the night and began banging on the door of the
closed railroad station.

"Is anyone there? Please. Open up. *Please!*"

Longarm set his things back down onto the baggage
cart and ambled down the platform. He removed his hat
and cleared his throat to draw the woman's attention.
More like a girl than a woman really. She was young, although it was hard to guess her age between the poor
light and a layer of heavy makeup that gave her a
raccoon-eyed, ghostly appearance in the flickering
lamplight.

She jumped with fright at the sound, then relaxed a
little when she saw a stranger standing there.

"The station seems t' be shut down for the night,
miss."

"But I have to catch the next train. I simply must!
When will the last one come?"

"Sorry, miss, but it pulled out, oh, five minutes or so
back."

He'd thought she was pale before. Now she looked like she would pass out. Her expression was one of raw fear.

"Oh, God!" Her eyes rolled up and her knees gave way, and she sank down onto the rough boards.

Longarm bent and scooped her into his arms. He carried her over to the baggage cart and set her carefully onto it. She was a fairly tall girl, but he doubted that she weighed a hundred pounds. She felt like little more than bone with some skin stretched over it. That skin was pocked with gooseflesh and she was shivering.

"Here, miss." He quickly shucked out of his sheepskin and wrapped it around her.

That got him to shivering again, so he left her sitting where she was for a moment and roughly dragged his tweed jacket out of the bundle that he had so carefully prepared just moments earlier. The tweed gave little protection from the night chill, but in this case "little" seemed much preferable to "none."

He tightened the leathers on the saddle again. By the time he was done with that, the girl's eyes were open and she was peering at him. She still looked awfully frightened and she continued to shake and to shiver. He was not sure whether most of that was from her fear or from the cold of a mountain night.

"Did he send you then?" the girl asked, something that might have been a hint of defiance showing in a pursing of her lips and a slight lifting of her chin.

"Pardon me?"

"Banner," she said. "Did he send you?" There was a hint of accent in her voice. Irish, he guessed, although without a brogue. In her case, it was more a faintly lilting cadence to her words. "Are you to take me back to him?"

"Young lady, I'm just a fella that got off that last train. Are you in some kind o' danger?"

"Oh, sir, it's you that may be in the danger here and sorry for it that I am. You've been kind to me and I've brought you naught but trouble."

Longarm smiled at her. "No trouble."

"He will make trouble for you," she warned. "Better you should have this fine coat back and leave me to my fate."

His smile grew warmer. "Now that would be a terrible thing for me t' do to a lovely lass, wouldn't it." She was not lovely. Not really. Her hair was disheveled and her face painted and her eyes seemed to take up half of her face. No, she was not lovely. But then, that was a lie that no female ever minded hearing, never mind the truth.

"You are kind, sir, but it would not be safe for me to remain with you. Really."

"But I need your help," Longarm said.

"I, sir? I could help you?"

He nodded. "I don't know the town. Could you show me the way to a hotel, please?"

"Easily done. Just in the next block over. There are three to choose from."

"Would you recommend one?"

"The—"

He shook his head. "Better you show me," he said. "And come inside to warm up." The smile returned. "After all, I'll be wanting my coat back, and I couldn't possibly accept it back from you until I know that you no longer need it."

"But . . ."

"Please."

She relented. Hell, that was what she wanted to do anyway. She was frightened and she was cold and she did not want to be left alone here without a coat regardless of what she might claim. "I will show you."

"Can you walk or should I push you on this baggage cart?"

"I can walk, I think. But what if he shows up? Or his men?"

"Whoever this Banner is, miss, if he does show up, why, then, him an' me will have us a little chat an' then each go about his own affairs. That's all."

"I've no wish to bring you harm, sir."

"Nor will you." He helped her onto her feet, then again picked up his carpetbag and saddle. "Lead the way if you would, please."

Chapter 5

The heat coming off a pair of potbelly stoves in the hotel lobby was more than welcome. Longarm quickly set his carpetbag and saddle down and unbuttoned his jacket to let the warmth reach his body, and spent a few moments standing beside the stove near the doorway while he warmed up.

There was no sign of anyone behind the desk, but someone had to be up and about or the stoves would not be so well fired.

"Looks like we need t' find the bell an' ring for some help," Longarm said.

"It's . . . they know me here. I will get him," the girl said. She turned and walked away.

She was still bundled to her ears in Longarm's sheepskin, but in the much better light inside the hotel, he could see that she had red hair and freckles. He guessed her age to be somewhere in her early twenties. Her face was too angular and thin to be pretty, but she might come close to it if she ever scrubbed away all the powder and rouge that made her look like she belonged . . .

Longarm grunted and nodded to himself. That was stage makeup she was wearing.

The girl disappeared into the back of the hotel, then returned a moment later. "He'll be right out." She unbuttoned Longarm's coat and returned it to him. "Thank you for the use of this. It helped greatly."

"I'm glad," he told her.

Longarm heard the sound of a door closing, and a sleepy-eyed middle aged man came out and stood behind the registration desk. "Good evening, sir. Or good morning. Which is it?"

"It isn't all that late," Longarm said.

The clerk grunted and reached behind him to pluck a key off a rack of them. The rack was mostly empty. "Here. You can pay tomorrow. I'm going back to bed. I don't feel good. Sorry." And he was gone, leaving the key on the counter.

Longarm shrugged. The girl looked uncomfortable. "Are you all right?" he asked.

She nodded, but he did not believe her. She said, "I'm sorry if . . . I don't want to be the cause of trouble for you, sir. I thank you for the use of your fine coat and I shall be leaving you now."

"Back out in the cold?" he said. "What good would that do? And what about the people you were running from? Wouldn't it be better for you to stay in here until the next train leaves?" He looked her up and down. There were no pockets in the dress she was wearing and she had no jewelry that he could see. "How do you intend to pay your fare tomorrow?"

"I hadn't actually thought that far ahead, don't you see."

"Well, I believe that. I'll tell you what. You can share my room . . . I gather your reputation won't be much the worse for that . . . then in the morning we'll see what we can do about your transportation."

"You are a kind man, sir. And I shall do anything you wish by way of thanking you for your help." She looked him in the eyes—he noticed now that her eyes were hazel, almost gold—and repeated, "Anything."

"That isn't what I had in mind," Longarm told her. "You're havin' troubles. I can help. That's all I meant."

She gave him a disbelieving look and tossed her head. "If you say so, sir."

"I do." He picked up the room key. "You seem to know your way around here. Can you tell me where this room is?"

The girl took the key from him and glanced at the tag on it. Then she picked up his carpetbag. "Follow me." Longarm retrieved his saddle and followed her upstairs to a room on the third floor.

The room was small, with a wardrobe, a washstand, and one rather narrow bed. Longarm set his things in the wardrobe and removed the tweed suit jacket. "Can I ask you a personal question?"

"Yes, of course." The girl began unbuttoning her dress. She wasn't wearing much under it. But then, she did not have much that needed covering. She really was just skin and bone.

He grinned. "What's your name?"

"Oh, God. I didn't tell you? No, I suppose I did not. Sorry." She extended her hand. "Diana Drury."

"Custis Long," he answered, accepting the handshake.

"And a pleasure it is to meet you, Custis."

27

"My friends generally call me Longarm, Miss Drury."

She gave him a skeptical look, quite obviously checking his hands and arms to see what it might be that prompted such a nickname. "All right. And I am Diana."

"Good enough. One more thing, Diana."

"Yes, L . . . uh, Longarm?"

"I'm not in the habit of taking advantage of folks," he told her, "so your virtue is safe with me tonight."

"I am no virgin, in case you hadn't guessed."

"I understand that, but even so. You don't have to pay your way here. I wouldn't feel right about it. On the other hand, there isn't room enough for us to do anything but sleep in this one bed. I can promise that I won't molest you if you'll not molest me in the night."

Diana laughed. "You are a nice man, Custis Long." She removed her dress and hung it carefully in the wardrobe. She was knobby and pale, and he had seen mosquito bites that were larger than her tits.

"Would you do me a favor, Diana?"

"Of course. I told you it's anything you want. Anything at all."

"Wash your face. I want to see what you really look like."

"Oh, you don't want that."

"Please."

"If you are quite sure." She went to the washstand and poured a little water into the basin. There was a dish of soft soap beside the basin. She used that and a washrag to get rid of the caked-on layers of powder. It took her a while to do it, but when she was done she looked years younger and immeasurably nicer.

"Thanks," Longarm said. He had been sitting on the foot of the bed watching while she was busy at the washstand.

Diana turned and hugged her arms around herself. "Do you want to know something funny? I have been standing here in my altogether for all this time and didn't think a thing about it. After all, I've been naked in front of strangers more times than I could count. But now all of a sudden, without my makeup, I feel naked. I . . . it is a strange sensation. I really don't know what to make of it."

"The makeup was a mask between you and the world," Longarm suggested. "Something you could hide the real Diana behind. I'm sorry. I didn't mean to take anything away from you."

"No, it's all right. Could I have one of those little cigars? Would you mind?"

"Help yourself."

She did and he lit it for her. Diana sat on the end of the bed, beside him but not touching him.

"Tell me about yourself," he suggested.

"There is not that much to tell. My mum and my daddy died when I was eight. No one wanted me. Then a man came round the orphanage offering work for nimble fingers. He took six of us girls on a big ship. We sailed to New York and worked in a factory there sewing shirts.

"When I was fourteen, another man bought me and brought me here to the West. We've traveled from town to town. Doing . . . shows."

"Shows?" Longarm asked.

"On stage. Having sex. With men. Women. Whatever."

"I see."

"I told you that I am no virgin. I meant it."

"Couldn't you leave him?"

"And go where?" she asked. "To do what? All I know how to do is sew shirts and have sex. Nothing else."

"Can you read?"

She shook her head. "I've never been to school. But I would like . . . someday I would like to be my own person. Do you know what I mean? I would like to get up in the morning, not the afternoon. I would like to walk in grass and see the sunlight reflecting on water. I would like to be a person, not just a thing."

"Everyone has that right," Longarm told her.

"Oh, sir. You really believe that. But you don't know. You do not know how precious it is to be your own self."

Longarm took Diana's hand and the two of them sat there in silence for a time until they finished their smokes. And for a considerable amount of time after that too.

Chapter 6

Longarm stripped down, but only as far as his balbriggans. Diana may have seen and done more than
Longarm could imagine, but he did not want her to
think he intended to take advantage of her need. He
would readily admit to being a horny sonuvabitch, but
he hoped no one would ever find him to be an unkind
one.

"Ready for bed?" he asked.

"Yes. Whenever you are."

He stood and crossed the room—it only required two
strides—and opened his Gladstone. He brought out a
bottle of rye and pulled the cork. "Do you mind?"

The girl gave him an odd look, but shook her head.

"D'you want some?"

"No, thank you."

Longarm took a pull from the bottle, let it soak in his
mouth for a moment, swallowed, and had another small
one. The flavor pleased him and the warmth of the
whiskey spread through his belly. He inhaled deeply

and seated the cork back into the bottle with the heel of his palm.

When he looked up again, Diana was naked. She lay on her back, her hands clenched into fists and held at her sides. Without the makeup, she looked young and almost innocent despite her nakedness.

"Scoot over, darlin'. You aren't leavin' me much room there."

"I'm sorry," She slid over until he thought she was going to fall onto the gritty, mud-smeared hardwood floor.

"I didn't mean t' throw you out o' the bed," he said. He eased down rather gingerly onto the other side. Springs creaked and the mattress sagged, but when he stretched out there was room enough, if just barely.

"Are you all right there? Got enough room, do you?"

"Yes," she said in a small and, he thought, frightened voice. The truth was that she did not have room enough. Neither of them did. Diana's hip was angular and her elbows sharp and he could feel both digging into his side.

"Tell you what," Longarm suggested after taking a moment to ponder the situation. "Let's us roll onto our sides. You face over that way. I'll face to this side. Maybe there'll be more room that way."

"All right."

He managed to roll awkwardly onto his side. Diana did the same so that they lay back-to-back.

"Comfortable now?"

"Yes. At least it is a little better. Sir?"

"Longarm," he corrected, then laughed. "If we know each other well enough to spend the night together, then I think it's only right that we call each other by name."

"Yes. Of course. Longarm?"

"Yes, ma'am?"

"You really meant it, didn't you?"

"Meant what?"

"You really meant it. About not fucking me, I mean."

"If I say somethin', little lady, then I mean it. You can count on that." He felt the bed shake very slightly. It took him several moments before he realized that the girl was crying. Longarm sat up and swung halfway around so he faced her. "What's wrong, child? Are you scared? Don't worry. I won't let nobody hurt you."

"It isn't . . . it isn't that. God knows I've been hurt enough that I ought to be used to it by now. It is just . . . just now you called me 'ma'am.' And 'little lady.' "

"Yes. What of it?"

"I am quite accustomed to being called 'bitch' and 'cunt' and 'meat.' But I have never in my whole life been called 'ma'am.' Not until this very moment."

Longarm reached for a handkerchief, realized that he had no pockets, and settled for taking the corner of the sheet and using it to wipe her eyes and scrub away the tear tracks that glistened on her cheeks.

"Oh, sir. I am sorry."

"Nothin' to be sorry about, little lady. You're doin' fine. Now lay back down an' get you some sleep. Tomorrow morning we'll get you away from . . . what 'd you say that fella's name is?"

"John Banner,"

"He's the fella bought you outa the sewing shop?"

"No, that was another gentleman. He didn't treat me all that poorly. I would have stayed with him. I did stay with him even though I could have run away if I wanted to. Not that there would be any point in that. I have no money. No friends. Nowhere to go."

"Well, now you have a friend, and you and me are gonna figure this out in the mornin'."

Diana took the end of the sheet from him and rubbed it over her face and wiped her eyes with it.

"D'you mind if I ask you something?" Longarm said.

"I would do anything for you, sir. You can ask me or order me or do whatever you will with me."

"Lo—"

She giggled. "Oops. Longarm, I mean."

"You say you wouldn't run away before for a lot o' reasons. What changed to make you want out now?"

"Mr. Banner. He won me in a card game and he is a . . . a very cruel man. It is not enough for me to give my body to whoever he tells me to. Now he wants . . . Mr. Banner wants me to have sex with a donkey. He wants to sell tickets and have me fuck a donkey and then be the prize in a raffle in the same show. I just . . . it is too much, Longarm. Too much." She shrugged. "So I've run. If they catch me, they shall have to kill me because I will not do his show with the donkey."

"You say he intends to sell tickets for this?"

"Oh, yes. He already has. He hired a barn, some sort of arena thing where they let dogs and cocks and badgers fight. Mr. Banner is terribly excited about the money

34

he can make with this idea. Except . . . I will not do this. I am firm about it. I shall not."

"No," Longarm said, "you damn sure won't. Now go to sleep, girl. Tomorrow could be a long day."

Chapter 7

It was not the most comfortable night Longarm ever spent, but it was far from being the worst. The only thing he really minded was having a hard-on practically the entire night through. Diana had a firm and resilient little butt, and Longarm was all too well aware of it being pressed firmly against his all night. All too well of the warmth that came off it. It was like sleeping with a small, soft heater. Except this heater, if he rolled over onto his other side . . .

Damn the girl for saying she would do *any*thing for him. She was naked. She was available. She was driving him crazy.

But he'd said he had no intention of touching her and he meant it. Diana had no idea what it was like to be something more than an object, and Longarm was not, he absolutely was not, going to treat her like one.

She kept him awake for a long time, though, thinking about it and feeling his pecker throb. Dammit!

It was well past dawn when Longarm woke. Diana sat upright at the first hint of movement from him. He suspected she had already been awake but had lain without moving until she was sure he was awake too. She was a timid little thing and reminded him of a young fawn, skittish and wary but unable to defend itself against fang or claw.

"Good morning. Are you hungry?"

"Good morning, sir."

"I asked are you hungry."

"I don't want to be a bother to you, sir. You have done more than enough already."

"Huh. Not half enough is more like it. Does this place have a good restaurant?"

"It has a restaurant, yes, sir, but I would not be knowing how good it is."

"I thought you knew this place well."

"Oh, I've been here many times, sir, but no one has ever wanted to be seen with me in a public place. Not, well . . . considering."

"There's a first time for everything, Diana. Put your dress on and let's go downstairs. I'm famished."

The girl looked nervous and uncertain at first, but Longarm insisted that she hold her chin high and the hell with what anyone thought. If any of the other diners even noticed Diana, they did not react, and certainly no one objected to her presence.

"I been thinking," Longarm said when the plates were cleared away and they were sitting over cups of strong coffee. "I got a little discretion about things, an' I think I'm gonna wait until tomorrow t' get a coach west. Do you mind?"

"Me, sir? Oh, it would not be for me to say."

"I don't wanta do anything that would upset you or hurt your feelin's, girl."

"Anything you do is all right with me, sir. Anything. And I mean that, I truly do."

"Then I think we'll wait until tomorrow to leave. For now I'd like you t' prepare a note for this John Banner you was telling me about."

"You are . . ." Her eyes began to fill with tears. "You will be sending me back to him, sir?"

"Not damn likely. Don't be thinking anything like that. I just want you t' help me with something."

"Whatever it is, sir, even if you do decide to send me back, I will do it for you. But if you ask me to write this note . . . sir, I canna read nor write. I'm sorry."

"Then have I your permission to write out a note and send it to him?"

"Yes, of course, sir."

Longarm summoned the waiter and asked for writing materials. A few minutes later, he sat up and carefully rolled the blotter over the single page he had just written. "I'll read this to you, Diana, but I don't want you t' worry yourself. You're known at this hotel an' by now Banner prob'ly already knows where you are. So you and me are gonna tell him something he already knows an' add a little to it. Here is what I've wrote down on this page.

"Mr. Banner. I recovered certain property of yours last night and understand she is scheduled to appear in your show this evening. I am enjoying what you might consider salvage rights, but will deliver her to the theater this evening at the time you desire. Please send me directions to the theater and an admission ticket, gratis, so I can take in the entertainment. I apologize for any inconvenience you may have suffered, but am pleased to be able to retrieve your property."

Longarm took Diana's hand and looked into her eyes. "Don't worry yourself about what I said. I won't let nobody hurt you. That's a promise."

She appeared to be frightened and uncertain, but she nodded and said, "All right, sir. May I ask you something, sir?"

"You're callin' me 'sir' again."

"Sorry."

"It's all right. Now what is it you want t' ask?"

"You used a word there. 'Gratis.' What is the meaning of that word, sir?"

"Free. It means free of cost, that's all."

"And you would be wanting a ticket for yourself?"

"That's right. But don't worry. I want Banner to think that his show will be goin' on. That don't mean that it will be, mind you. Just that I want him and his men t' be there."

"If . . . whatever you say, sir."

Longarm had their waiter fetch a bellboy. Diana gave the boy instructions about where to deliver the note; then Longarm signed for their meals and led Diana into the lobby.

"We got some time t' kill until dark," he told her. "I'd like t' do a little shopping if it's all right with you."

"Of course, sir."

"Then take my arm, please, an' we'll go see us some sights. I want t' buy you a warm coat. D'you have clothes wherever it is you been staying?"

"I have some costumes, but not much in the way of real clothing. Not really any decent dresses or things like that."

"Then let's go get you fitted out with some proper things, ma'am."

"Oh, but I haven't money to pay for these things and I do not want to be a burden to you, sir." She seemed to have abandoned the use of his name. "Sir" was simply more comfortable to her.

Longarm grinned. "Don't fret yourself. We'll charge these purchases to Mr. John Banner."

Diana's eyes became wide. "You can do that?"

"Watch me!" Longarm squired her out the door on his arm like she was the finest lady in town.

Chapter 8

Longarm drew the proprietor aside while Diana admired some ready-made dresses that hung on a rack at the side of the store. He bent down and whispered in the gentleman's ear, "The lady is Mr. Banner's . . . how can I put this . . . she is Mr. Banner's 'special friend.' Mrs. Banner doesn't know about her and Mr. Banner wants to keep it that way. D'you get my meaning there, friend?"

"Oh, yes, but . . ."

"But what am I doin' with her? Mr. Banner can't be seen walking with her in public, so I do that. I'm what you might call an assistant to Mr. Banner. A personal assistant."

"Oh, I see."

"Mr. Banner has broad business interests, you understand, an' when he finds someone he likes t' do business with, he does a lot of it. That includes makin' his local purchases."

"Really? Oh, my!"

Longarm figured he had the storekeeper hooked now.

The thought of doing more business. Big business. Yes, sirree. In truth, though, Longarm had no idea if John Banner had other interests—probably he did not or he would not be scratching for peanuts with his fuck shows—nor did he know if the man had a wife hidden away somewhere. Longarm's interest right now was Diana Drury and her wardrobe.

They chose two very handsome traveling dresses, four light housedresses, shoes, some sturdy underthings, a hat, toiletries, and a suitcase to carry it all in. When Diana was finished with her shopping spree, she was as excited as a kid at Christmas, practically hopping up and down with it.

The bill for all that came to a whopping forty-seven dollars and eighteen cents.

The proprietor packed everything into the suitcase and Longarm told him, "Charge that to Mr. Banner, please. He'll be around later on t' settle up with you. He's kinda busy at the moment."

"Yes, I heard he is putting on a . . . a very special show at Hansen's fight pit this evening."

"Very special," Longarm said with a leer and a wink.

The proprietor looked across the counter at Diana, then at Longarm; then he blushed.

"That's right," Longarm said. "You gonna be there tonight?"

"My wife would . . ." The man's expression hardened and his chin came up. "I will be there. I wouldn't miss it for the world now."

"Good," Longarm said. "We'll see you there." He gave a little emphasis to the word "we" in that.

The proprietor blushed again. And looked like he hoped he would be the lucky patron who ended up getting Diana for the night when the donkey was done with her. Longarm could not quite understand that, sloppy seconds being one thing but . . . after a *donkey?* Each to his own, of course.

The storekeeper got his mind back onto business and quickly said, "You will sign for these purchases, I presume."

"Yes, of course." Longarm accepted the sheet the man handed him and took his time about perusing the list of items and the stated cost for each, then checked the arithmetic to find the total. "This looks right," he said. "Everything in order."

He borrowed the use of a pencil and scrawled, "For John Banner. Signed, John Law."

The gent glanced at the sheet and smiled. "Very good, Mr. Law. I will see you tonight."

"I'll put a word in for you with Mr. Banner," Longarm said, cutting his eyes toward Diana, who was quite oblivious to this whole thing.

"Yes. Thank you. Thank you very much."

Longarm picked up the suitcase and offered his elbow to Diana so he could squire her back to the hotel for a late lunch.

Longarm wiped his mouth and dropped his napkin beside the plate. "I dunno about you, girl, but I'm full as a tick on a hound dog's ear."

Diana giggled. "That's funny."

Longarm smiled. "Did you know that you have a

very nice smile? With a dimple. Right there." He very lightly touched her cheek near the corner of her mouth.

The girl turned away, blushing. "Thank you."

"Look, Diana, I don't want t' be bossy, but I think we'd be wise to keep you off the street this afternoon. We should stay out of sight, so t' speak."

"Anything you say."

"In that case, I'm thinkin' we should go upstairs an' take a snooze." His grin flashed. "I know I didn't get much sleep last night, How 'bout you?"

She shrugged.

"Then let's go." He stood and assisted Diana with her chair and her wrap, then gave her his left arm to steady her on the stairs. The desk clerk, a different fellow from the night man, seemed surprised to see Diana being treated as if she were a lady, but a cold glare of warning kept his mouth closed when they passed by the desk in the hotel lobby.

At the room, Longarm unlocked the door and held it for Diana to enter, then bolted it closed behind them.

He looked at the narrow little bed and said, "We might could get something bigger if we raised a fuss with that fella downstairs."

"No, please, this . . . this will do. If you don't mind, that is."

"It's fine by me, but can I ask why?"

"That man on the desk. His name is Tom, and he . . . he has used me before. I don't want to be a burden to you, but . . ."

"Fair enough." Longarm crossed the room—it only required two steps—and opened the window to let some fresh air in, then began stripping off his clothes, "Don't

46

fret," he said. "I'm just tryin' to get comfortable here so's we can get some rest."

"Believe me, that could not worry me." But he thought she looked relieved nonetheless,

Longarm stretched out and was asleep within seconds.

Chapter 9

Something—some sound or movement or he knew not
what—brought him awake. He was alert, but not
alarmed. He remained very still, listening for some tell-
tale that would determine if he should grab the .44 from
its holster on the bedpost.

He heard . . . the creak of springs. Soft breathing.
The squeal of an ungreased axle and the clop of a
horse's hoofs from the street below. But no danger.
No . . .

"Sir? Are you awake, sir?" The whisper was so soft
he might have imagined it.

Longarm's eyes fluttered open. Diana's face was
inches away from his. She was peering at him intently.
She had something pleasant—anise seed perhaps—on
her breath.

"You're awake," she said in a normal voice.

"Yeah. Are we late?" He knew they were not. The
sunlight was still strong beyond the light gauze that covered the open window.

Diana shook her head. "I just . . . I'm scared."

Longarm touched her shoulder. Her flesh was cool, and she was trembling just a little. "I told you. I'll take care that you aren't hurt."

"Would you . . . do you know what helps settle me down? What I would like to do?"

"What's that."

"I would like to hold you."

"Sure, darlin'. I'd like that too."

"In my mouth."

"Par'n me?"

"I would like to hold you in my mouth. It would please me. Settle my nerves, like."

"You can't be . . ."

"It's like a pacifier to a bairn."

For a moment he thought she was saying something about a barn. Then he remembered. Bairn. Kid.

"Please?"

"I, uh, sure."

Diana smiled as sweetly as if he had just given her a present. "Thank you."

The bedsprings creaked again as the girl shifted position, turning so that she was curled tight against his side with her cheek resting on his belly.

She lightly touched him. Longarm's pecker reacted, snapping to attention as sharp and straight as any shavetail lieutenant could have done.

"Lovely," she said, sounding quite happy about it. "It is so big." She giggled. "Maybe I should have chosen the donkey instead."

"Look, I . . ." He tried to sit up. Diana pushed him back flat on the bed. "I was only teasing you."

"Okay, but if . . . oh, my!" She took him into her

50

mouth, her warmth surrounding him for just a moment. Then she released him again. The air reaching wet flesh seemed suddenly chill.

Diana slipped her hand beneath his balls and cupped them in her palm as if weighing them. She squeezed very gently and ran her fingers over the top of his cock while her tongue made a matching trip up the other side.

"Lovely," she said again.

She puckered her lips into a pout and touched them to the tip of his cock, then sucked him in so that the bulging purple head was drawn inside her mouth. It was warm in there and very soft. Very welcoming.

Longarm's breath caught in his throat at the feel of her as Diana ran the tip of her tongue around and around his glans while his cock remained inside her mouth.

"Nice," he said. He meant it. Diana did not try to push things too fast or too hard. She gave him time to absorb the sensations she was giving him. "Very nice."

Diana toyed with the sensitive area between the base of his balls and his asshole, scraping a fingernail over it, rubbing the pad of a forefinger over it, finally shifting so that she could lick him there. The feeling was so intense that Longarm thought he was going to squirt on her hair.

Just barely in time to avoid that embarrassment, Diana pulled back and once again took him into her mouth, this time acting as if she intended to stay there until he came.

Longarm cupped the back of her head and said, "Wait."

"Is something wrong? Am I not pleasing you?"

"Not likely. You please me plenty, little girl. I was just thinkin' t' give you some of it too. Roll onta your back so's I can get on top."

"Oh, no. You mustn't do that."

Diana must have seen his confusion because she quickly added. "It is that I have the clap."

His eyebrows went up and he could feel his erection subside. "Banner?"

"He does not know, the son of a bitch."

"But you're sure you got it?"

Diana sniffed and laughed. "I should certainly hope so. God knows I tried hard enough."

"You tried to *get* it?"

She giggled again. "'Deed I did. I hate him, you know. He always gave me lambskins so I shouldn't have diseases. Except I threw them away. And I was always extra-special helpful with any man who had a discharge from his penis. That is one of the signs of it, you know."

"Yes, I know."

"Oh, I fucked and fucked all the laddies who might have the gon . . . the gon . . ."

"Gonorrhea," he suggested.

"Yes. Thank you. And I've got it. Have had for several weeks now, I think."

"And you've given it to Banner?"

"I certainly hope so."

"Good Lord," he said.

"You shouldn't worry, though. I never used my mouth on anyone who had it. I didn't want to waste an opportunity, you see. So my mouth is clean. It's my

52

vagina that is diseased. Would you like to use a lamb-skin just to be sure?"

"Do you have one?"

"No, do you?"

He shook his head.

Diana shrugged. And resumed sucking his cock.

Damn, but the girl was good at it.

The hell with it. Longarm closed his eyes and dropped his head back to the pillow under his neck while Diana slurped and gurgled down below.

Chapter 10

The daylight was fading when Longarm woke again. He was rested and thoroughly refreshed, the hour or so of sleep having very little to do with that. He sat up, the movement jostling Diana on the undersized bed.

"What's wrong?" She bounced onto her feet. "Are we late?"

"We're fine." He reached for a cheroot, bit the twist off, and spat it onto the floor. He rummaged in his vest for a match to light the smoke, then began getting dressed. "Hungry?"

"Do we have time?"

He nodded, then looked at her and grinned. "Hell, the show can't go on without us."

Diana gave him a stricken look. "Please. I don't have to . . . I don't, do I?"

"Sorry. I should've thought before making so free with a joke. No, you ain't gonna have t' do anything. You're just the ticket to this John Banner fella's downfall. You get me inside the door with him. Nothin' more."

"Thank you. I don't mean to complain. Really I don't. I just . . ."

"It's all right, Diana. I should've thought. I apologize."

"Thank you."

"Getting back to the original point," he said, "we got time for supper before we go find this dog pit. Here in the hotel be all right with you?"

She nodded and finished dressing while he took a piss in the thunder mug; then Longarm gave Diana his arm and escorted her down to the dining room.

Both of them ate lightly, Longarm because he might need to be light on his feet, depending on how many men Banner had and how loyal those men were to their boss, and Diana, Longarm guessed, because she had little appetite due to nerves. She was pale and obviously frightened, but she seemed determined to go through with whatever Longarm had in mind.

When they were done Longarm signed for the meal—he wondered if he could palm the room and other charges off on Banner like he had Diana's dresses—and handed their room key to the man on the desk, a different fellow this time.

"Ready?"

She nodded.

"Then lead the way, please."

It was full dark when they stepped out onto the sidewalk. The chill of a Colorado high country evening had settled in, and the sky was clear as springwater.

Lights showed in the windows of half-a-dozen businesses along Silverthorne's main street and there was the tinkle of a piano—either a player piano or one mighty damn accomplished piano player—coming from a nearby saloon. When they passed by the batwings, Longarm could smell the sharp scent of beer wafting out into the night. It smelled good enough to make his saliva run.

"It is down here," Diana said, making a turn off the dimly lit main drag and into the shadows of a side street.

Longarm paused as if to draw on his cheroot, but in truth so his eyes would have another moment to adjust. He took Diana's hand and led her toward a dark, low roof ahead and to their right. He was fairly sure this would be the right place. There were a good two dozen men standing around outside drinking and smoking, and he could hear the buzz of several dozen conversations beyond the low doorway.

An elk hide was nailed over the portal to act as a door. When he pushed it aside, he was hit with a wave of heat and odor, the heat from dozens of bodies packed into a small space and the stink of too many unwashed men in that space.

Longarm's nose wrinkled and his nostrils flared. He could smell the copper scent of blood here too. He briefly wondered how many dogs had died here for the amusement of the patrons.

Not tonight, though. Tonight, instead of an open pit to fight in, the center of the arena, sunk a good six feet belowground, was occupied by a sturdy wooden platform.

Carbide lamps with polished reflectors were placed around the circumference of the ring, making the platform awash in bright light.

A burro, its fuzzy ears laid back nervously, was tied to a stanchion at the back of the ring.

Longarm did not know how they had gotten the little

fellow down there, unless someone had lifted him down by hand. There was no gate or ramp for animals the size of a burro to come and go.

When Diana saw the burro, she moved closer to Longarm, pressing her hip tight against his. He could feel her discomfort.

"Don't fret," he whispered into her ear. "I won't let nobody hurt you."

Then he straightened upright, extending his hand with a smile as a tall, distinguished-looking gent approached.

This had to be John Banner, he thought. In the flesh.

This, Longarm thought, was going to be a piece of cake.

Closer inspection indicated that Banner was perhaps not quite as distinguished a chap as he seemed at first blush.

The points of his shirt collar were beginning to fray, and there was grime under his fingernails. The heavy gold chain that ran from one vest pocket to another was not gold, as it was supposed to appear, but had begun to rub off, displaying a base metal of some sort beneath a golden wash or plating.

The man was at least as tall as Longarm, slender, with a pencil line of mustache across his upper lip. He had salt-and-pepper hair parted in the middle and a day's growth of beard that needed shaving.

Banner did not display a firearm, but there was a bulge under his right armpit that suggested a shoulder holster there. And suggested as well that the man was left-handed. It was a thing to keep in mind.

So was finding out how many men Banner had with him. Diana did not know, although Longarm had asked her. "Lots" was as close as she could come to telling him. "He gave me to many men, but I never knew which of them had me as a right of their employment and which paid for the privilege."

Now Banner smiled coldly when he looked at Diana. And why not? She was the evening's star attraction. The man looked Diana up and down, then shifted his attention to Longarm.

"You are a man of your word," Banner said. "You have her back to me in good time. Splendid little piece, isn't she? She hates that I can always make her come, but I can. How about you, sir? Did she howl and scratch and go wild when you finished?"

"No," Longarm said. "I got t' admit that she did not."

"No matter. A whore's feelings are never of importance. All that counts is if she gave you a good ride."

"She did that."

"Fine. Where did you find her, may I ask?"

"She was at the train station," Longarm said truthfully enough. "She missed the last one out. I'd just got off." He smiled again. "My good fortune, wouldn't you say?"

"And mine. Now if you would turn my property over to me, please . . ." He held his hand out to Diana.

"That reminds me," Longarm said. "This show you got planned for . . . was it your 'property,' is that what you said?"

"Yes, indeed. She belongs to me, sir. You, uh, you are not expecting compensation for her return, are you? After all, you had the exclusive use of her ever since you found her, and you are being given access to the show. I've even reserved a front-row seat for you, right down there where you can see and hear everything that happens."

"That's fine," Longarm told him. "What about this show you have planned? What's gonna happen there?" He nodded toward the platform in the bottom of the dog pit and toward the burro that remained tied there.

"You know good and well what will happen," Banner said.

"Yeah, but she told me she didn't want t' do it."

"Bah!" Banner exclaimed. "It doesn't matter what she wants or what she says. She belongs to me and if I say she will do it, then she will. I promise you."

"Belongs t' you, does she?"

Banner nodded. "Bought and paid for, sir. Bought and paid for."

Longarm took a drag on what was left of his cheroot. It had burned down to little more than a nub. "Interesting you should say that. You ever hear of the Fourteenth Amendment to the Constitution o' these United States?"

"What the hell does that have to do with anything? Now hand her over, sir. I will not stand for any extortion, I can assure you." Banner looked past Longarm toward someone on the upper tier of seats in the arena. He nodded.

Help, Longarm thought, was on the way. Not that it was unexpected.

"What we have here," Longarm said, "is a case of involuntary servitude. That ain't legal, mister."

Banner's face clouded and turned a dark, mottled red. "You can take this 'legal' bullshit and shove it up your ass. Sideways."

"Yeah, well, I might consider that except my boss would get pissed at me."

"I don't care—"

"Just so's you know," Longarm told him, "I'm a deputy U.S. marshal an' I am placin' you under arrest." He let go of Diana's hand and reached around to the small of his back for his handcuffs.

John Banner held his right hand high as if in surrender. But his left hand strayed close to the lapel of his suit coat.

Longarm's lips stretched into a thin smile that held not the least hint of mirth. "You'd best not try it, friend."

It was good advice, and John Banner should have taken it.

Instead, he clenched his right hand into a fist, obviously a prearranged signal, because there was an immediate scurry of shoes on the wooden flooring as some of Banner's bullies leaped to their boss's aide.

At the same time, Banner's left hand darted beneath his coat.

Longarm abruptly shoved Diana out of harm's way, then dropped into a crouch, his blue-steel .44 suddenly in his fist.

"Don't!" he cried out.

Chapter 11

Don't, hell! Banner did.

The response was not unexpected, and it was obviously planned, likely had been used effectively more than once in the past. Let the men behind cause a distraction with their loud clatter of footsteps while the boss took care of things with his quick gun.

Except Longarm was quicker. And he was neither distracted nor intimidated by the strong-arm boys behind him.

Longarm's Colt spoke before John Banner's pistol cleared the lapel of his coat.

The bullet smashed through Banner's thorax and blew out a good four inches of spine at the nape of his neck before it disappeared somewhere inside the dog-fighting arena.

Banner went down instantly, as limp as a discarded scarecrow.

Longarm spun around, still crouching, Colt held ready, to meet the rush of Banner's henchmen. There were four of them, he saw, but they held cudgels instead of pistols. They came to a halt when they saw the muzzle of Longarm's .44.

The arena was in pandemonium. Men cursed and scrambled to get away from the gunfire. Diana lay on her side, curled into a tight ball, whimpering and shaking with terror.

Longarm rose to his full height and kept his Colt leveled on Banner's four men while he pulled out his wallet and flipped it open to display his badge.

"Deputy U.S. marshal," he said. "This man resisted arrest. What about you?"

He did not have handcuffs enough for all four of them, so he let the crowd disperse—within moments he, Diana, the four men, and the burro were the only living creatures in the place—then had the four step down to the front row nearest the fighting pit. They had to climb over their dead boss to get there and walk in the blood that was trickling down the steps.

"I don't know how you got that burro in there," Longarm told them, "but now you are gonna get him out. And you ain't gonna hurt him doing it."

"We thought we'd, uh . . . we thought we'd take it out as feed for the dogs," one of the men volunteered. "The owner of the pit said we could do that."

"Now I'm saying you can't. The burro comes out, alive and unharmed. D'you understand me?"

"Yes, sir."

"Do it." Longarm reloaded the .44 from some loose cartridges he customarily carried in his coat pocket, then pushed the revolver back into his holster. He bent then and picked Diana up, cradling her in his arms and sitting down in one of the arena seats so she ended up sitting across his lap. He held her and rocked her, wiping her face and stroking her hair. After a few moments, she sighed and snuggled down against his shoulder. That seemed a good sign that she was returning to normal. Or whatever "normal" was for her after all the abuse she had suffered at the hands of uncaring men.

Down on the floor of the pit, Banner's assistants managed to pick the burro up and set him over the retaining wall onto one of the stair aisles. From there, the fuzzy-eared animal was able to scramble up and out the rest of the way on his own.

"All right, mister. What now?"

"Now you boys an' me are gonna walk over to the Silverthorne jail. You'll be charged with . . . shit, I ain't entirely sure yet what-all you'll be charged with. Me and my boss will have t' work that out when I get back from where it is I'm going right now. Until then, you boys can set in the jail here. On my way back through, I'll pick you up an' carry you down to Denver with me. Any argument with that?" Longarm glanced pointedly at John Banner's very messy body. There really was an awful lot of blood that had drained out of him.

"No, sir. No argument."

"D'you think you can walk now, Diana?"

She nodded. "I'm fine now. Honestly."

"All right." He set Diana onto her feet and stood up beside her. To the men in the pit, he said, "We'll all of us be goin' over to the jail now. Any of you wants to pull gun or try an' make a break for it, you go right ahead. Just keep in mind that if you do, you'll end up like him." He gestured toward Banner.

He expected no trouble from them. And he got none.

65

Late that morning, his prisoners locked the town jail, Longarm accompanied Diana to the train depot. She had little in the way of luggage, but she did have money. Longarm had given her everything that was found on John Banner's body, less the cost of burying the son of a bitch. The sum was substantial.

He handed her a note. "This here is the address of a friend o' mine."

"I can't read it, you know."

"I know, but just hand the paper to the driver of the hansom cab. He'll take you there. When you get there"— he reached into his pocket—"when you get there, give Miz Whipple this note here. It kinda explains things." "It doesn't . . ."

"No, dear, it don't tell any details. Just that you're needing honest work. There's always work that needs doing in a big restaurant like she runs. There's washing t' be done and food t' cook an' orders t' take or to deliver. Miz Whipple will give you work and a place to stay. You'll be safe there and you won't hafta do nothing that you don't want to. Ever. You understand? Nobody's gonna make you do anything you don't want, not ever again. When I get back to Denver, I'll look you up. Maybe we can have dinner together or something."

"I think I would like that," Diana said.

"An', Diana."

"Yes?"

"When you get down there, there won't be nobody who knows anything about your past. Nobody. Even if you run into somebody that you . . . that you was with before . . . you just look them in the eye an' tell them they's mistaken, you ain't the girl they thought you was. And mean it. They'll back down and accept that. If you mean it when you say it, they will accept it every time." He smiled. "If it happens, which it might not."

Longarm leaned down and gave the painfully thin girl a light, brotherly kiss on the forehead. "It's time to find your seat. I'll see you when I get back to town."

He turned Diana over to the helpful attentions of a porter and a conductor, tipped his hat to the girl, and left the depot to get on with his job.

Chapter 12

Putting Diana on the train to Denver made Longarm miss the first stagecoach west, and the second—there were only two each day—would not leave until afternoon. He deposited his Gladstone and saddle with the manager of the express office, enjoyed a leisurely lunch and signed over a voucher for his lodging at the hotel, then went back to the express office to wait for the westbound stage to roll in.

Something Custis Long had wondered much of his adult life was just why the fuck waiting room benches had to be so damned uncomfortable. All of them. It didn't matter where you were waiting or what for. Stage, train, or doctor's office, the seating was going to be lousy. He pulled out a cigar and decided that when he got back to the office, he really ought to ask Henry to look it up and see if there was a law about that.

Eventually, thank goodness, he heard the rumble of wheels and the jingle of harness, and the depot manager stuck his head into the waiting room to tell Longarm and two other gents that the coach to Glenwood Springs and points west had arrived.

"We're loading your luggage now, folks. Soon as we change to a fresh team, you'll be under way."

Once the stage line man had gone back into his office, Longarm fished his Ingersoll out and checked the time. He was almost disappointed to see that the coach was within seven minutes of being spot on time.

"You can come out an' board now," announced a thin, middle-aged fellow who was long overdue for a shave. He carried a coiled whip in his hand. It was a badge of office of sorts, declaring to all and sundry that he was a stage line jehu. King of the road and captain of his dry-land ship. There was no more respected being on the planet—barring the occasional preacher or schoolmaster—than a stagecoach driver, and kids for three counties around would know their names and their reputations.

Longarm deposited the stub of his cheroot in the pan of sand the stove sat in, then trailed the other passengers outside into the late afternoon sunlight. At this elevation there, he could already feel a nip in the air. Come nightfall, it would be downright chilly.

The other two gentlemen, one representing a Denver brewery and the other a hardware salesman from Ohio, climbed into the coach, leaving the hard and narrow middle bench for Longarm as the comfortably padded but rear-facing front seat was already occupied by a young woman and a girl of twelve or fourteen or so. Sisters, Longarm guessed, although why they would be traveling unescorted he did not quite understand.

Not that it was any of his business. He nodded and

touched the brim of his hat as he settled onto the seat and tried to find a comfortable position there.

There was no back on the middle seat, just the very lightly padded bench long enough to accommodate two passengers and just barely wide enough to perch on without causing actual damage to the human anatomy. Longarm despised having to sit on middle benches.

"Ladies," he mumbled, determined to be polite.

The older girl raised a gloved hand to her face and pointedly looked away. The younger giggled and gave him a big-eyed stare, until the elder gave her an elbow nudge that Longarm was not supposed to see.

The coach rocked from side to side when the jehu and the shotgun climbed into the box, and a few moments later there was the riflelike crack of the jehu's whip.

Longarm did not have time to brace himself at the sudden lurch forward, and he damn near toppled backward onto the lap of the gentleman from Ohio.

That fellow gave Longarm a rather annoyed shove to set him upright again.

The kid was grinning at his discomfort, and he thought he spotted the edge of a smirk behind the glove of the older girl.

Not that he had any interest in these kids.

But he could feel the sting of embarrassment anyway.

It was, he thought, going to be a long ride west.

Oh, shit. Deputy United States Marshal Custis Long was in deep trouble.

All afternoon he had been thinking about Diana Drury. Actually, what he had been doing was bluntly regretting that he had allowed her to blow him.

The girl had gonorrhea, for crying out loud. She told him so herself. The question now was, was that disease confined to her pussy, or could she transmit it by way of her mouth?

If there was anything Longarm did not want—well, there were quite a number of things he could happily do without—high on the list was the clap. How embarrassing. Hell, how painful!

And now . . . this.

As the afternoon wore into evening and the stagecoach rumbled on, Longarm began to feel a crawly, nasty, utterly insistent itching. In his crotch.

His pecker itched. His balls itched. His belly itched so badly he wanted to rip his britches off and claw at himself with both hands.

Yet those two young girls sat directly in front of him, so close their knees frequently bumped his whenever the coach jolted over a rock or a root, unaware of his acute discomfort. And awake.

Dammit, if they would at least drop off to sleep, he would be able to sneak in a scratch.

Just one good scratch. That was all he needed to make it feel better.

But, no. His whole crotch was afire, as if a cupful of stinging ants had been dropped in his lap, and those genteel young ladies sat, wide awake, chattering behind their fans and their handkerchiefs, oblivious to Longarm's misery.

He squirmed. He shifted back and forth. He wished he could leap out of the coach and go screaming away down the road while scratching with both hands.

He . . . sat there. Anguished. For hour after endless

hour. Worrying about what disease or diseases Diana might have given him.

Itching!

It was not until morning, when the young ladies left the coach at Glenwood Springs, that Longarm was able to escape to some privacy inside a privy at the stagecoach relay station.

He carried a basin of clean water and a washcloth into the privy with him, dropped his trousers, and gave himself a thorough inspection, then bathed his cock and balls in cold water.

That relieved the itching.

It was not until twenty minutes or so later as he was finishing his breakfast that he realized the whole damned thing had been a simple case of excessive worry.

There was nothing wrong with his pecker. Diana had not infected him with anything. And he was no longer itching.

Imagination! Shee-it.

"Everybody who's continuing on west, come out and climb aboard," the jehu announced, standing up and putting his hat on. "We got miles to make and I'm not waiting for you."

Longarm dutifully dropped a quarter on the table to pay for his meal and went outside into a cool and lovely new day.

Chapter 13

Longarm had no idea what Toynbee, Colorado, looked like even though he was standing on a street corner in the middle of it, the only passenger who left the coach there. Also, the only passenger who was awake at one o'clock in the morning when the stagecoach pulled into town.

Along about sundown, he had transferred to the Adamson and Sons Express line at DeBeque and headed north onto the flats that rimmed the Colorado River.

The coach, with two snoring salesmen aboard, would be driving on to Twin Rocks, which was somewhere up in the Black Sulphur River country. It was a trip Longarm would likely have to take too, but first he wanted to get a look at things at this end of his assignment. The Twin Rocks part of it could come later.

Not knowing how things would shake out here, he had not used the privilege of his badge to provide for his passage with Adamson and Sons. It was entirely possible that he would not want anyone with the stage line to know who he was, considering that they were the principal suspects in the sabotaging of the railroad.

Now he collected his saddle and luggage and asked the hostler who was handling the change of horses where he could find a room for the night.

"There's a hotel in the next street over. Got to warn you, though, them folks don't change their sheets regular. That's what the passengers all say. If you're partial to a clean bed, you might ought to try Miz Wallace over that way." He hooked a thumb in the direction he meant. "She rents out her rooms for board. She knows what time our coaches run too, and if she's got a room to let, there will be a lamp in the window. If you don't see no lamp, though, don't wake her. You'll just piss her off and not get a room anyhow. If'n there's no lamp, you best turn around and come back to the hotel."

"Thanks for the advice, friend."

"Any time." The hostler yawned and smiled and went back to buckling the fresh horses into harness.

Longarm picked up his gear and started walking toward Mrs. Wallace's boardinghouse. He was in luck. There was a lamp burning in a front window.

Longarm normally woke in an instant, coming awake completely and suddenly. Not this time.

He heard the door open, heard footsteps on the oak flooring inside his room. He thought about reaching for his revolver. Somehow it seemed too much trouble to move. It was bad enough having to open his eyes.

Finally, groggy and his head pounding, he forced his eyelids open.

"Oh, 'S you, Miz Wal'ce." He closed his eyes and

flopped deep into the feather pillow that came with this heavenly soft bed.

"Are you all right, Mr. Long?"

He heard the question as if it came from far away.

"I was beginning to worry about you, you've been asleep so long," she said.

He grunted softly, but did not risk opening his eyes again. Hell, if he did that, he might wake up.

"I see that you haven't died, so . . . I apologize for walking in on you like this. Go back to sleep. I suppose."

There was the soft sound of creaking floorboards and then a door latch. Longarm was gone at virtually the same moment that the door closed.

He woke up the second time feeling like he was coming off a three-day drunk. No, more like a week-long bender. He was parched. His mouth tasted like it was stuffed with cotton. His eyes ached. And dammit, his pecker was itching again.

A look outside told him that he had slept the clock around and then some. It was morning. At least, he thought east was that way. Surely, he hadn't slept so long that he was looking at a setting sun.

Shivering and convinced that he was close to starvation, Longarm pulled his clothes on, then flipped the loading gate open on his Colt and gave the cylinder a slow spin before buckling the revolver in place. Just checking that it hadn't been tampered with while he was . . . away.

"Well, good morning," Mrs. Wallace said when he got downstairs. "I was beginning to think you would sleep another whole day through. All my other boarders have had their breakfast and gone."

"Sorry," Longarm said. "I didn't mean t' cause you no trouble."

"Trouble? Anything but. I'm charging you for board as well as the room, you know, and you haven't eaten a thing yet. Trouble? You're giving me a fine profit. Now sit down. I'll get you something to eat."

"Lordy, that sounds fine." His stomach was rumbling, and the lingering scent of cooking bacon made his mouth water so hard it was difficult to swallow it all away.

"Coffee?"

"Please. An' after breakfast I'd appreciate directions to a barbershop where I can get a shave an' a bath."

"Of course. Now do sit down at the table there. I didn't believe you could sleep much longer, so I've saved some food for you. Sit, sit."

"Yes, ma'am."

Chapter 14

When Longarm walked out of the barbershop after bathing, he felt damn near human again. Ready to start the day all fresh and . . . well, not early perhaps. But ready to start the day.

He took a deep breath, enjoying the scent of the bay rum the barber had splashed on, then took a look around Toynbee. Not that there was so very much to see. It was a town of perhaps fifteen hundred souls, built spread out along the rim of a deep cut that was not deep enough to be a canyon but, at forty feet or so with sheer walls, was too deep and well defined to be a mere gully.

There were no buildings at the bottom of the cut— that would have been suicidal since it was water, a lot of it at a time, that had gouged the earth here—but there were garden plots laid out down there to take advantage of the subsurface irrigation. Likely, Longarm thought, those produce gardens were the reason Toynbee grew here. It wasn't just everyplace out here in this arid country that a man could farm like that. And when the next gullywasher came through and scoured the ground bare again, well, the only damage would be to some vegetables, and probably to the wooden stair steps that had been built here and there along the near rim so folks could get down to tend their plantings.

There should be enough produce out of those gardens, Longarm thought, to supply the needs of tables for a good many miles around. This was cow country, so there would be ranches scattered here and there. There were men digging ore of some sort out of the ground over at Twin Rocks. And now there would be railroad construction crews who needed to be fed. Likely, he thought, the men who were raising those vegetable crops would have a good market for everything they could produce.

Apart from that, there was not much of interest in Toynbee. Adobe brick was the preferred building material, the town being far from the good timber that could be had in the mountains to the east and south.

There were—he counted—six saloons and two cafés to serve the people here. Obviously, the good folk of Toynbee had their priorities in order.

There were two churches. Three general mercantiles. A school. Several commercial buildings. A bank. A smith. A pharmacy. A tailor. A livery that also served as the relay stop for the stagecoach line. And a fairly large wagon park behind the livery. An otherwise vacant plot beside the wagon park had piles of stacked ties already cut and creosoted. There were also some long, low stacks that were covered with canvas sheeting. Rails, he suspected, waiting to be spiked in place. There was also a small building that looked like a railroad depot but without a railroad to serve, even though there were the beginnings of a roadbed in front of it. He could see where the railroad was intended to begin, but as yet it had not.

All in all, Toynbee seemed to be a quiet, sunbaked little town.

At this time of morning, which Longarm was embarrassed to realize was past ten o'clock by the time he got ready to start the day, there was activity along the main street, and over at the schoolhouse he could hear the sounds of children at play. You couldn't find a town much quieter or more easygoing than this, he thought.

A sign on the side of one of the downtown buildings indicated the home office of the TOYNBEE & TWIN ROCKS R.R. on the top floor of the two-story structure. A staircase on the outside of the building led up to the railroad offices.

Longarm wanted to know where that office was. He was sure it was information he would need sooner or later. But not now. He was not yet ready to show his hand to the people who were trying to stop the construction of the railroad.

With that in mind he walked down to the stagecoach office.

"Can I help you, mister?"

"Just wanted to check your schedule. I'll be wanting to go over to Twin Rocks. Maybe later today."

"You're too late to do it today. This is a small line. We only run two coaches, the one you came in on last night from DeBeque, then another that runs between here and Twin Rocks. The Twin Rocks coach leaves here at six o'clock every day but Sunday. There's no service on Sundays. It gets into Twin Rocks about two in the afternoon, changes horses, and makes the return trip. Usually gets back here about ten-thirty or eleven at night. Three dollars and a half one way or six for the round trip."

Longarm grunted.

"Are you a businessman, mister?"

"No, I'm just . . . looking around." He smiled and tugged on the ends of his mustache.

"Ah. Investor, are you? Well, they tell me there's money to be had over there. They're going to build a railroad, you know. Once that gets laid, it will be easier to bring ore out and machinery in. They say property values will jump as soon as that happens."

"A railroad, you say?"

"Sure. That's what all this is for." The man waved his hand to indicate the piles of building materials stacked outside his wagon yard. "They say they'll start laying track as soon as the right-of-way is ready."

"Really?"

"Sure. They got bridge builders and road graders working on it now. Should be ready to hire in the gandy dancers and start laying actual track in another couple months, or so they tell me."

"But what is the sense of building a railroad with no rail connection at either end, just the one lone section laid out between the two towns?" Longarm asked.

"You haven't seen the country between here and Twin Rocks yet. It's all cut with washes and gullies. That makes it awful hard to freight equipment in or raw ore out. You may have noticed that we don't have a mill around here to process ore. Everything has to be hauled out in wagons. A railroad will take care of that problem.

Besides, there's supposed to be another line building through from Denver all the way to the Sierra Nevada. When that gets in, our little spur line can connect to it and put us right in the thick of things."

"You sound eager," Longarm said. "I would have thought a stagecoach line employee would resent a railroad coming in and taking business away from you."

"Friend, I may act as an agent for the line, but this livery business is mine. I'll still have that no matter what the railroad does. The railroad should actually bring in more business to this part of the country. More than it takes away, I'm thinking. I expect the progress to be good for me and my business."

Longarm grunted, mulling over what the stage agent said. After a moment, he nodded. "Three-fifty, you said?"

"For one way, yes. The coach leaves at six o'clock every morning. Six sharp, mind you. If you're late, you have to wait for the next day."

"Thank you. You've been a big help."

"Any time, mister." The man turned away and ambled away, disappearing inside his barn.

A very big help, Longarm thought as he walked back into the business district. But a puzzlement. He had expected resentment at the coming of a railroad. Instead, what he found was approval, at least from this one man.

Of course this fellow was only an agent employed by the stagecoach line. It could be that the owners, presumably someone named Adamson and his family, had harder feelings.

The answer to that would have to be found at the Twin Rocks end of the line.

In the meantime, he wanted to gauge the opinions of the general populace.

And he knew the best way to learn that.

Longarm lengthened his stride, moving purposefully now toward a likely-looking saloon in the next block.

Chapter 15

"Dealer takes one," said the gent to Longarm's left.

"I'll open for a nickel."

"I'll see that."

"I'm in and raise a nickel. Dime to you, Long."

Longarm looked at his cards and shook his head. The hand was nothing but crap. He folded the cards together and tossed them onto the table. "Fella over at the livery barn said all that material piled over there is for a railroad," he observed. "What is that all about?"

"Progress," the dealer said with a grin. "There is a transcontinental building out this way, and now there will be this Toynbee and Twin Rocks line to connect with it. Between them, they should put us on the map. Open up markets we couldn't ever hope to reach otherwise."

"Sounds like a good thing for the town," Longarm said.

"A good thing and then some," added a beefy man with a toothbrush mustache. "Like George said, this railroad construction is going to be a godsend for all of us already here and bring in a whole lot more folks too."

"Lot more folks, lot more business," the fellow at Longarm's right elbow put in.

"In both directions. Freight in, freight out."

"What sort of freight would be coming out of here?" Longarm asked.

"Raw ores coming out of Twin Rocks for processing down at Grand Junction," George, the dealer, said. "Farm produce from right here. Beef on the hoof from all over this part of the country. We aren't as dead and dreary as you might think just from looking at us."

"You have yourselves a nice little town here," Longarm said.

The gent with the mustache grunted and said, "Give us five years and take another look. We won't be so little then. We're on the upswing. Count on it. I'll raise another nickel, by the way. I mean . . . we are playing poker here, aren't we? How about it, Leonard? Are you in?"

Longarm stood and hitched up his britches. "Excuse me for a minute. I need t' take a leak. Can I bring another pitcher with me on my way back?" He reached for the nearly empty pitcher of beer and poured what remained there into George's glass. Then Longarm turned and headed for the bar.

If there was so much as one solitary soul in the town of Toynbee who had reason to object to the coming of the railroad, Longarm had not been able to find him. He'd spent the entire day—what was left of it once he finally got up and around—talking with folks. Asking polite questions. Passing the time of day. He had not yet heard the first unpleasant comment about the proposed railroad construction.

Preparations were well under way for the arrival of the tracklaying crews, and advance crews were already busy, he was told, marking and grading the right-of-way, while others were building short trestles that would be needed to bridge the many dry arroyos that cut across the rolling landscape here.

Saloon keepers and tradesmen seemed to be uniformly pleased with the new business those crews brought in with them. Several were talking about plans for expansion. No one seemed to be complaining.

Not that Longarm had had time to speak with each and every resident of the town. But he certainly thought he had a fairly good sense of the townspeople's sentiments now, and those were strongly in favor of the arrival of the rails.

Whatever problems there were did not seem to be coming from this end.

He had his supper at the boardinghouse—and listened to the other guests more than spoke—then made another trip through the saloons, here playing a few hands of cards, there standing with a mug in one hand and a cigar in the other. He did not try to force the direction of the conversations he could overhear. Again, there seemed to be no undercurrents of resentment that he could detect.

About ten, he was at a blackjack table. The dealer was a plump woman with hair like brass curls and a face that would have been pretty if she washed off half a pound of powder and some of the kohl around her eyes. The eye makeup made her look like a chubby raccoon.

"Quitting so early, honey?" Her lashes fluttered and she tipped her chin down so she was looking up at him through them. "Maybe you ought to stay. Maybe if you did stay we could . . . play." She made it sound suggestive as hell. Longarm was not fooled. What this one wanted was his money, not his body.

"Next time," he said as he pushed a half-dollar tip across the table to her.

The eyelashes fluttered again, but her smile was mechanical, and he could see that as far as she was concerned he was no longer of interest. No more money, so no more charm.

Fair enough. He wished her well, her and everyone else here.

Longarm picked up his coins—he was slightly ahead for the night—and headed back to the boardinghouse. He had to be up early in the morning if he expected to make that one coach per day over to Twin Rocks.

Chapter 16

Once he turned off the main street through town, it was as black as the inside of a whore's heart. He hoped there were no dogs sleeping in the street, or he would trip over them for sure.

He pulled out a cheroot while he walked, nipped the twist off the end with his teeth and spat that out, then dipped two fingers into his vest pocket for a match.

He paused and scratched the match afire, bending his head to bring the cigar down onto the flame. He puffed gently on the cheroot to get a coal started, then shook the match out and tossed the blackened sliver away. The smoke tasted good on his tongue, and he could feel the lingering warmth of a glass of rye whiskey pleasant in his belly.

Life, he thought, was good. Except for a faint itch that persisted around the head of his cock. Damn that girl anyway. If there was a doctor in Twin Rocks, maybe he should have a word with him about the likelihood that he was coming down with something.

Longarm took a moment to get his bearings—he did

not want to blunder into a hitching post or trip on the edge of a sidewalk, and it seemed even darker to him after the bright flare of that match—and set off again toward the boardinghouse.

He heard a faint scuffling to his left. Very soft. Cats maybe, or raccoons?

The sounds came toward him.

Longarm turned his head in that direction and strained to see, but his fire-blinded vision was useless.

He heard a grunt. That was a man, dammit, not a bunch of four-legged prowlers.

Instinctively, Longarm ducked, raising a forearm to defend his head from—

Shit!

Someone charged into him. He could smell garlic on the sonuvabitch's breath and could hear the huff of labored breathing.

A hard blow landed on his forearm. Better there than on his head, however, where it had been aimed.

Longarm dug blindly with his other hand, sending a fist crushing into soft tissue, a belly maybe or under the short ribs.

His attacker cried out and took a step back, so Longarm pressed forward, shoulders hunched and chin down. He could not see, but he could damn well fight. He threw another punch, this one connecting with nothing but air. Dammit, if he could only see . . .

Blinking rapidly in an effort to clear his vision, he listened for a moment. Heard the scrape of leather on gravel. Pulled back just a little.

Something very solid crashed into the side of his head and he nearly lost his balance. He was rather dimly aware that his teeth had clashed together and he had bitten off the end of his cheroot. That bit remained in his mouth while the lighted end had fallen away somewhere. For some reason, that seemed terribly interesting to him.

He felt dizzy and disoriented. Thought he was going to be sick to his stomach.

That would serve them right. He would puke all over them, whoever they were.

They? As in more than one? He thought so, although he could not remember why he thought that. But he was sure there were at least two.

He was going to beat the shit out of them too. Just as soon as he got up again.

Up? When the hell had he fallen down?

He could not remember doing that, but . . . but he was on his knees now.

He felt another hard knock on the back of his head. The sound of it was dull, almost hollow. That was supposed to be funny, wasn't it? Hollow noggin. Nothing in there.

He was not laughing.

He was lying facedown now, although again he did not recall just how he got there.

He could feel rough hands pulling at him. Rolling him onto his back.

The gun. His Colt. Where was it?

He tried to draw the revolver, but his hand was not cooperating very well. It refused to do what he was telling it.

A hand other than his own pushed rudely into his right-hand pants pocket.

Longarm tried to cuss the son of a bitch who would do a thing like that, but no sound came out of his mouth. The best he could manage was a faint exhalation of what precious little breath he had left.

He could feel someone tugging his coat open.

"You! Get away from that man."

The voice was loud. And shrill. And female.

Longarm heard the crunch of feet on gravel and then pounding footsteps as his assailants fled.

That was the last thing he remembered.

Chapter 17

Longarm's head spun like a kid's oversized top—well, it felt like it did anyway—and it was a good thing he was already sitting down or he would have fallen off the side of the bed.

He blinked rapidly, trying to bring his vision into focus. It took a while.

"Where . . . ?" He got no answer. There was no one else in the bedroom.

Whose bedroom? He did not know that either. He did not recognize it. Certainly, it was not the room in Mrs. Wallace's boardinghouse.

His head was throbbing and when he, oh, so very lightly investigated, he could feel a goose egg on the back of his head. The lump hurt like a sonuvabitch and he winced when he touched it.

He had no recollection of where he was or how he got here. It took him two tries to stand upright, and then he was unsteady and swaying.

"Hello? Is anyone here? Hello?"

There was no answer, and he had the impression that

the house was empty. Small too, he judged. The ceilings were low and the rooms small.

He made his way out of the tiny, unkempt bedroom to find himself in someone's kitchen. Through another door there was a sparsely furnished parlor. That was it. Three rooms and a small porch off to the side of the kitchen.

The place was not much, but it was home to someone. Someone who apparently had little in the way of money. The few furnishings were old, cheap, and much used. Strands of horsehair leaked from the one upholstered piece, a sofa that was so thoroughly used that he could not be sure if the pattern of the cloth originally had been ordinary flowers or fleurs-de-lis.

There were no pictures on the walls to give him a hint of who his host might be.

Holding onto the door frame to keep from losing his balance, Longarm made it into the kitchen and slumped into one of the two chairs that faced a tiny table that sat in the middle of the room.

There was table service for one in a drying rack beside a copper tub.

And a coffeepot sat on the range. Lordy, what he would give for a cup of coffee.

Longarm stood and walked with exaggerated care to the range. He hefted the coffeepot and smiled when he discovered that it was heavy. Smiled even broader when he touched the side of the pot and found it to be warm even though there seemed to be no fire in the stove. He wondered just how long he had been unconscious.

He fetched the cup from the drying rack, and was

pouring himself some coffee when the latch on the side door lifted.

Longarm's hand flashed to his waist . . . and came up empty. He still wore his clothing, including his gun belt, but his revolver was gone. His holster was empty.

He braced himself. If this was one of those men who'd jumped him last night, about all he could do was to splash them with hot coffee and follow up just as hard and fast as he could manage. Which, he suspected, would not be all that damned hard *or* fast. He would do what he could, though. He might be taken, but the bastard who did it would have to work at the chore.

The door swung open and a chubby, middle-aged woman stepped inside. She carried no weapon more threatening than a shopping basket. She stopped when she saw him standing there in her kitchen.

For a moment, he was worried that he had somehow broken in and put himself to bed when she was out. Then she smiled. "Good morning. Afternoon, I should say. Last night you were babbling, then all of a sudden you went out like a candle in a hurricane. I was beginning to worry about you."

Longarm set the coffeepot down and tried to concentrate. This woman looked vaguely familiar. Yet he thought he had never seen her before this moment. "I . . . excuse me, please, but who are you an' how did I get here?"

She laughed and set her basket down. "Sit down. I'll finish pouring that coffee for you and then explain. You don't remember me, though, do you?"

He shook his head—a big mistake; he winced from

the pain the sudden movement caused—and said, "Sorry. I don't."

She laughed again. "Just a second." She stepped into the bedroom and opened a cabinet, taking out a brassy wig that she pulled on. "Of course I don't have my makeup on, but perhaps this will help."

"Oh, hell. O' course. You're the blackjack dealer from last night. But how'd I get here?"

The woman took him by the elbow and guided him to a chair in the kitchen and set a full cup of coffee in front of him before she answered. Damn, that coffee tasted good.

"I found you lying in the street when I was on my way home last night. You came around a little, enough to help me get you onto your feet and inside. You were practically at my front door anyway. You'd seemed a very nice man at the table, so I brought you inside and put you on the bed. It was clear enough what had happened. We've had some robberies in town recently. Thump and grab. That sort of thing. You must have been thumped pretty hard."

Longarm gave her a wry grin and gingerly touched the back of his head. "Yeah, you could say that. Did you find my gun?"

"I don't think those men had time enough to take anything. I scared them off when I yelled at them. I found your gun. It's in the bedroom on top of the chest of drawers. You have your wallet. It fell out of your coat, so I put it back. I didn't go through your pockets to see if they took anything."

Longarm was still wearing his britches. He felt of them and discovered there was no thin lump where his

96

barlow pocketknife should have been. If that was the only thing that was missing, he could say that he'd come off mighty lucky.

His big question now was whether this was some random attempt at robbery . . . or if the stagecoach people had identified him and wanted him out of the way.

The woman said there had been some alley bashings in Toynbee recently. It could have been simply one of those.

Or it could be that some smart bastard realized those muggings would make a perfect cover for the deliberate murder of a deputy United States marshal.

He was not willing to lay a wager in either direction.

"Are you hungry?" his benefactor asked. "That's why I had to go out. I wanted to get some food in for when you woke up." She smiled. "How would ham and eggs sound to you."

"What are you, some kinda angel?" His mouth began to water at the mere mention of ham and eggs.

The fat woman's laughter filled the kitchen and she began building up the fire in her range preparatory to cooking a huge, sumptuous, mid-afternoon breakfast.

Chapter 18

Half a pot of coffee and a hot meal got Longarm on the road to recovery, but he still was groggy and slid in and out of full awareness. He did not go unconscious. Exactly. But he did tend to lose track.

"Look, honey, why don't you come back in here and lie down," the woman said. "You said you need to catch the next stage north, but that won't be until morning. Me, I have to get some sleep too. I got to work tonight."

"Work?" His head felt like his brain was stuffed with cotton.

"I deal cards at the saloon. Remember?"

"Oh, right. Sorry."

"It's all right, sweetie." Her name was Ella. She had told him her last name, but he could not remember it. It was an odd and rather disturbing feeling to be so forgetful about little things. "I'll wake you when I get back from work, okay?"

Longarm nodded. Gently. And let Ella help him up.

Things had come to a damned sorry state, he thought, when a fat middle-aged woman had to help him walk a dozen paces to the bedroom. Worse, she had to assist him with the buttons on his shirt. His fingers did not cooperate when he tried to take the shirt off by himself.

He balked when she got down to his drawers.

"It's all right, dearie," Ella said, giving that last garment a firm tug. "I've seen more pricks than Custer had Indians." She pressed him down onto the bed. "I didn't always look like this, you know. No, you wouldn't know, would you. Anyway, it's the truth. There was a time when I was quite a looker. Had the fellas lined up waiting for a few minutes with me. That's how I made my living to start with, see. I was a whore."

Longarm must have registered some surprise because she added, "Oh, it's true enough. I don't try and hide it. I ran away from home when I was fifteen. Fell in love with a sweet-tongued gentleman." She smiled. "He looked a little like you if the truth be known. Oh, he was pretty. He popped my cherry, then caught a stage out. I followed him. Caught up with him and lived with him the better part of two years. That's where I learned how to deal cards. Back then, I didn't need anything but a smile and a wiggle of my ass to make a living, though.

"Anyway, the bastard left me one awful cold winter. Left me not a bite to eat and owing rent. The landlord offered to take the rent out in trade. That wasn't so awful bad. It wasn't like I was a virgin or anything. And after that"—she shrugged—"one thing led to another. That same man set me up in a little house. He took most all the money, but he did treat me good. I was never cold nor hungry, neither one, which was a damn sight better than my sporting man ever done by me. That lasted until my looks started to go. I tried to stick with it, but the houses got seedier and the gents started to smell worse and all look the same. So I bought me some cards and spent a little time practicing the things I'd learned when I was young and pretty. And now here I am, lucky enough to have another pretty man in my bed. Now lie down and go to sleep."

Longarm very dimly heard the thump of a shoe hitting the floor, and then another. He heard a faint rustle of starched fabric and a series of small noises that he could not identify. Then the bed shifted alarmingly to one side. He thought the softly sprung thing would tip over, but it only sagged. Ella, he realized, was home from work and crawling into bed beside him.

He felt the bed shift again and heard a huff of exhalation, and the bedside lamp went out.

There was not really room enough for two in the narrow bed. Longarm tried to accommodate the situation by turning onto his side. He discovered that Ella was doing the same thing, probably also trying to make the most of the little space that was available. He found himself pressed tight against Ella's back in spoonlike fashion.

With her weight tilting the mattress toward that side, Longarm found himself rolling downhill just a little so that his chest rested on her back; his lower belly lay against her more than ample ass, and his thighs were tucked in against hers. He could feel every movement she made.

And she seemed to be moving quite a bit. Very small, subtle motions. Back and forth. Back and forth. Very softly. But rhythmic. Insistent. There was something about it that he thought he should recognize. Something . . . Shit! She was masturbating herself. Trying to get herself off with a finger or a candle or something.

"I ain't asleep, Ella," he whispered.

The movement stopped. "Sorry."

"Are you all right?"

"I'm fine," she said. "It's only . . . this is the only way I can unwind and get to sleep when I get home."

"You do it every night?"

"Sure. Unless I'm on my period. Does it bother you?"

"No," he said quickly. He was not sure that that was true, but it certainly was the proper thing to say under the circumstances. Not that the circumstances were proper. Not hardly.

"Do you want me to do you?" Ella offered.

"No," he repeated.

He heard her giggle. The bed moved when she did so.

"What's funny?"

"You say no, but I can feel your hard-on."

"I don't have . . . all right, maybe I do."

"It's all right, honey. You aren't scaring me with it." She giggled again. "But it feels like a good one." She shifted position a little, still lying on her side, but now with her butt pressed hard against him. "Here."

Ella reached around behind and took his cock in hand. She guided it forward, between the rolls of fat that were her ass and her thighs.

Longarm was almost shocked to feel her pussy clench hot and slippery around his shaft. It felt damned good.

"Don't be shy," she said. "Push. You aren't so big that I can't take it."

Longarm pushed. And Ella's flesh fully enveloped him. He lay on his side and so did she, and now they were connected at the crotch. Her body was hot. At least down there it was. In front of his nose, fat Ella smelled of perfumed powder and stale sweat. He was pleased enough that he could not smell her pussy.

But, oh, he could certainly feel.

He withdrew. Just a little. And pushed again. The sensation was magnificent.

"Do you like?" She shoved her butt back against him when he moved forward, drew away an inch or so when he pulled back.

"You know I do."

"Hold still for a minute."

"I don't know that I can."

"Trust me."

"If you say so." Longarm stopped thrusting and held himself rigid.

Ella pushed her butt back, taking him inside as far as he could go. Then she just lay there. Or appeared to.

But . . . he could feel . . . shit, he could feel her clasping his pecker. Clenching tight and letting go. Milking him. Driving him damn near crazy.

And there wasn't a hint of it that would have been seen had anyone else been standing right there beside the bed staring at them.

All of it was taking place inside her pussy.

Clenching tight. Relaxing. Again and again, until the sensations began to build. Build and then to overwhelm. Overwhelm to the point of exploding.

Longarm cried out and thrust forward convulsively as his jism spewed out into Ella's body.

He came so hard he thought his toenails were going to fly out like they were shot from a cannon.

He grabbed Ella's side, took a handful of belly fat, and hung on until the wild ride ended and he was able to lie back, exhausted. "Damn," he mumbled out loud.

"Not so bad, eh?" she said with a chuckle.

"Mighty fine," he agreed.

"I'm glad you approve. Now move back. Just a little. That's good. I need to clean both of us off, then I have to get some sleep. This has been a long day."

He yawned. "What time is it?"

"About four."

"Then let me up, please. I have a stage to catch and you'll sleep better with just you in the bed."

"All right, but you come back any time you like, dearie. You're always welcome here."

Longarm kissed her—not entirely a pleasant thought but it was the right thing to do—and crawled out of the warm and slightly sweaty bed.

He did indeed have a stage to catch, and this time he intended to be on it.

Chapter 19

The land north of Toynbee was brown, barren, and choppy. From a distance, it appeared to be flat. It was not. It rolled and tilted and was cut into a crazy-quilt pattern by ancient washes left by rare, long-ago rains. From the coach window, once in a great while Longarm could see a cow. He was more likely to spot a soaring hawk or a rattlesnake annoyed by the rumbling passage of the stagecoach wheels.

The thing that amazed him was not the fact that there were valuable minerals in the ground here, but that anyone had been looking to find them.

But then, in his experience, prospectors were mostly insane to begin with.

"Young man. You there."

"Yes, ma'am?" He removed his Stetson and placed it on his lap while speaking to the aging lady who was sharing the coach today.

"When will we stop for dinner?"

"I don't know as we will, ma'am."

The woman sniffed. He could not see her expression

behind the veil that hung down from her hat, but he could read annoyance in the way she tossed her head. "I have a delicate constitution," she complained. "I cannot be kept from my dinner."

"Yes, ma'am. I'll be sure an' tell the driver that when we stop t' change the horses."

"Would you?"

"Yes, ma'am," he said politely, not meaning a word of it. Still, he reflected, it was a good sign about the future of Twin Rocks if the high muckety-mucks at the mining companies were bringing their families in, as he judged to be the case with this lady. Men don't do that unless they expect to settle in for the long haul. Obviously, the people involved in the mining expected to be there for a long time.

The road to Twin Rocks paralleled almost exactly the roadbed that was being prepared for the railroad. Over the course of the morning, they passed two base camps where tents and stacks of timbers were positioned for the work crews who were building trestles to bridge the many arroyos.

There were armed guards posted at the camps, Longarm noticed, and more standing watch over the work gangs who labored in the dry heat.

They stopped about nine-thirty to exchange the team for fresh horses.

"Five minutes, people. We pull out again in five minutes, with ya or alone. It don't make no never mind to me," the driver said as he crawled down from his perch high on the quarterdeck.

"Ma'am," Longarm offered, "would you like for me

t' see could I find you a little something t' eat? A chicken leg or something?"

He heard that sniff again. "Consume something from this disgusting place? Certainly not."

Longarm rubbed his chin. He hadn't had time this morning to shave and it was pretty scratchy. Probably, he looked fairly disreputable, he conceded.

"Do not presume to speak with me again unless I first address you," the old biddy declared. "Manners." She sniffed. "You Westerners simply have no manners."

"No, ma'am."

She stood for a moment, looking around. Not that there was much to see. A sod-walled cabin where the station tender and his Indian woman lived. A large corral with some heavy-bodied horses standing hipshot in the sun. A well. A collection of storage sheds and some tarpaulin-covered stacks of feed. Everything was bleached of color by the relentless sun, but Longarm could see too that it all was tidy and in good repair. The station keeper knew his business.

"Young man."

"Yes, ma'am?"

"Where are the comfort facilities?"

"The what, ma'am?"

"The loo."

"Oh, you mean the shithouse," he said loudly. He wished he could see the face behind that veil, but the sliver of wattled neck that was visible under the veil was enough. It turned almost purple.

The old bat grabbed up her skirts and wobbled hastily out of sight behind one of the sheds.

Two minutes later, when the driver emerged from the crapper—which was in plain sight for anyone who bothered to look—the station keeper handed over the reins to the fresh team and held the leader's cheek strap while the driver climbed onto his perch.

"All set down there?" the driver called out.

Longarm did not want to disobey the lady in the veil by speaking up without her say-so.

He kept his mouth shut.

A few seconds after that, the driver yipped to get the team's attention. He cracked his whip and the coach lurched into sudden motion.

Longarm permitted himself a very small smile as he moved across to the forward-facing seat and propped his boots up. He pulled out a cheroot and lighted it with great satisfaction.

Chapter 20

Twin Rocks was not all that different from Toynbee. Except smaller. And dustier. And more raw.

The whole town looked like it had been built over the past weekend. Even the lumber had not yet had time to start weeping pine sap, much less weather to the usual gray patina.

The country here was flat enough to play billiards on if only someone would get rid of the buildings. The exception was a large pit probably eighty or ninety feet deep where men and mules labored to scrape pale dirt out of the ground.

Whatever they were mining here, there was a lot of it, but obviously the ore was a low-grade substance. Wagons hauled the stuff away in bulk and no one bothered to stand guard over them. Pilferage did not seem to be a problem.

Longarm walked over to the edge of the pit and took a few minutes to look it over. Scrapers taking ore out of the bottom loaded it onto sturdy wagons, which carried it up a roadway that wound around the inside of the pit. He judged the bottom to cover a good four acres or so.

"What is that stuff?" he asked a passerby.

"Borax," the man said. "Good quality too. Good purity."

"I didn't know there was any here."

The man grinned. "Neither did anybody else. Until now."

"Lucky for somebody," Longarm offered.

"The fella that made the find is named Tom Hartman, and you're right. He's a lucky man. He sold out just a month or so ago. Got his price and decided to go off and see the world. England, France, all them places. The new owner has big plans for this operation. Big expansion of the mine, a railroad, school, even an opera house, or so they tell me."

"That sounds like big plans to me," Longarm said.

"Yep. Talk is we should have ten, twelve thousand folks here by the time he's done."

"Ambitious."

"Yep. But that's the way a man gets ahead."

Longarm stuck his hand out. "Custis Long," he said.

"Pleased to meet you, Custis." The fellow shook Longarm's hand. "I'm Dan Hayward." He smiled. "I haven't meant to be nosy, but I'm what passes for a town constable here. I'm also a special deputy for this area, the county seat being all the way back in Toynbee where you just came from."

"Now how d'you know—"

"I saw you get off the stage. And before you ask, yes, I followed you over here. Wanted to size you up a mite. You look like you could be a gambler. Or some sort of fancy man, in which case I'd want to inform you that we already have enough whores. We aren't needing any more."

Longarm threw his head back and roared.

"Did I say something funny, Custis?"

"Yeah, Dan, you did, though I know you didn't mean to." Longarm pulled his wallet out and flipped it open to display his badge.

"Long. Are you one of Marshal Vail's dep . . . shit! You're the deputy they call Longarm, aren't you?"

"Ayuh."

Hayward grabbed Longarm's hand again and pumped it vigorously. "I've heard a lot about you, Long."

"Call me Longarm, Dan. All my friends do." He winked. "Some of my enemies too."

"They say you're hell on the hoof with a six-gun."

"That's a nice compliment but I don't know as it's all that true."

"You're still alive, aren't you? And you've had your share of scrapes and then some."

"All that is true enough."

Hayward grunted and let go of Longarm's hand. "I'm pleased enough to say that I've never had to shoot a man. Had to draw my pistol a couple times, but that's as far as it ever went."

"Then you are a lucky man, Dan."

"Where are you staying here, Longarm? Got a room yet?"

Longarm shook his head.

"Well, you do now. You can stay with my missus and me. Come along. We'll grab your gear and get you settled; then you can tell me what you're doing here and how I can help."

"Whoa, I can't just move in on you and your wife. That wouldn't be right. I can take a hotel room."

"Look behind you, Longarm. You see those big long tents over there? Those are what pass for hotels in Twin Rocks right now. They're like barracks. Just big, open cow pens with lousy food and high prices. The state of things here hasn't yet caught up with the needs of a couple hundred bachelors. I don't recommend you move in there. You'll be a whole lot more comfortable with me and Thelma." He smiled. "Best food in town too. Guaranteed."

"I hate to . . ."

"I insist. Really."

"All right, Dan. You talked me into it. Let me go fetch my gear from the stage office an' you can show me the way."

Chapter 21

Housing was in shorter supply in Twin Rocks than Longarm had realized. The constable and his wife lived in a place that would scarcely have qualified as a shack in a more settled location.

It was haphazardly built, divided into two rooms, and had a sun-rotted piece of canvas for a roof. Longarm could not see into the half that presumably was a bedroom. The living area held a table, a stove, a standing cabinet, two straight-backed chairs, and a rocking chair. The cabinet and rocker were obviously of fine quality. Everything else was cheap. The surprise was Mrs. Hayward.

Longarm guessed the constable's age at something in the neighborhood of forty or forty-five. He doubted that Thelma Hayward was out of her teens. The constable's lady was a statuesque six feet, buxom and blond. When Hayward dropped the news on her that they had a houseguest, her only reaction was to drop her eyes toward the floor and mumble something that Longarm could not hear. He supposed it was an acknowledgment of the introduction.

"Don't mind Thelma," Hayward said. "She's shy. Good cook, though."

"My pleasure, ma'am," Longarm said. The girl turned away, eyes still downcast, and went back to the pan of English peas she was in the middle of shelling.

"We can carry these chairs out to the porch," Hayward said. "Be out of Thelma's way."

"That'd be fine." Longarm set his saddle and carpetbag down beside the door and took the offered chair, carrying it back out onto the little open platform that Hayward called a porch. At least, with the angle of the sun and the time of day, it was in the shade. The heat out there would likely be brutal in the middle of a summer day.

Once they were outside, Hayward nudged Longarm with his elbow and whispered, "She don't say much but she'll do any damn thing I tell her to." He winked and gave a little chuckle. "Anything."

"You're a lucky man," Longarm said politely, not meaning a word of it. Thelma Hayward seemed more like a servant than a wife. But then, what the hell did he know about it, being mostly undomesticated himself.

"Yes, I am. Got a good job. Got that to come home to. Yep, I'm one lucky cowboy."

"That's what you did before you pinned on a badge?" Longarm asked.

"Right," Hayward said. "I've rode for just about every brand on this side of the Rockies. Not that there's so very many outfits over here on the west slope. I've rode for near all of them that are here, though. My last job was with the JO. I liked that just fine. Wouldn't have quit them but I took a bad fall. Was chasing some calves and my horse tried to jump an arroyo that was about two foot wider than the silly sonuvabitch could manage. I ended up with a broke leg and a back that still pains me. Joker gave me my choice. I could stay on the ranch as the cook's helper, or I could move into town here and become the constable. So . . . here I am."

"Joker?" Longarm asked. "Who would that be?"

"You never heard of Joker? I'm surprised. Joker Owens is who I mean. He owns about half the country in these parts. He's working on owning the rest."

"No, I don't know of him."

"Stay around here and you will. There isn't much happens in Dolan County that doesn't come back to Joker, one way or another."

Longarm pulled out a cheroot, offered it to Hayward, and when the constable refused, bit the twist off and lit it himself. "Speaking of the state of affairs over here," he said, "what d'you know about the trouble the railroad crews are having trying to get their road built?"

Hayward fingered his chin and pondered his answer before he spoke. "I know the railroad people blame Jess Adamson and the stage line. But then, everyone knows that much. God knows, Jess complains about the railroad loud enough to everybody that walks by, and the railroad people complain just as loud, each one saying the other is at fault."

"What d'you think, Dan?"

"Me, I don't know, Longarm. The good thing is that it ain't my place to worry about it. All I'm responsible for is the town. Whatever happens along the road between here and Toynbee is not my worry."

"You said you're a county deputy too," Longarm reminded him.

"Special deputy. If the sheriff calls on me, I'll do my duty. But you won't find me looking for trouble outside my own bailiwick."

Longarm grunted and puffed on his cheroot. Nice fella, this Hayward. Just what a peaceable little town like Twin Rocks needed. Most of the time. But a first-class lawman he was not, and likely never would be.

Whatever trouble there was here and whoever was responsible for it, it would be up to a professional like Longarm to take care of it.

"Thelma will have something on the table here in a little while," Hayward offered after a moment. "You're going to like supper. I guarantee it."

Chapter 22

Supper was . . . adequate. Barely. The dishes were attempts at being fancy but fell short of the intended effect, and the portions were woefully small, probably because Dan Hayward was developing a paunch that strained the buttons on his shirt and overhung the buckle on his gun belt.

The coffee, however, was good. Longarm liked a good cup of coffee.

Thelma Hayward served the men, hovering over her husband and seeing to his needs like a mother hen. Longarm had no idea what the girl was like when she and Hayward were alone here, but with him in the house altering their normal routine, she rarely glanced in his direction, did not meet his eyes once, and never spoke a word directly to him.

"You can see we don't have much in the way of extra space here," Hayward said when the meal was done and they—and their chairs—were outside on the porch again.

"Cozy," Longarm said, trying to put the best possible face on things.

"Small," Hayward said with a chuckle. "Good thing it isn't size that makes a home happy."

"So it is," Longarm agreed. "Will you have one of these cheroots now?"

"Yes, thanks."

They both lit up and sat with their chairs leaning back against the front of the shack.

"My point is," Hayward went on, picking up his flow of thought again, "we want you to take the bedroom. Thelma is laying out a pallet beside her stove. That will be fine for her."

"Which, if I have the heads counted correctly, leaves one bed short," Longarm said.

"Not really. The town can be lively after the work shift. You know how it is with workingmen. They want a drink, a whore, play some cards. Like that."

"Of course."

"I spend my nights making the rounds and keeping the peace," the constable said. "The sort of thing a night marshal or a deputy should do, but here in Twin Rocks I'm all the law there is so I have to do most of my work at night. I won't get any sleep until the saloons empty out and the men go back to their barracks. Then I'll come home and crawl in with Thelma for a few hours."

Longarm nodded and blew some smoke rings. They were quickly distorted by a faint breeze. "That's fine," he said, "but be careful who you're snuggling up to. I'm not putting you and your missus out of your own bed." He quickly held his hand up, palm outward. "No, Dan, I'll not hear any argument about that. I'm used to sleeping on the ground as much as in a bed anyway, and I simply am not gonna take your bed. I'll be just as pleased with the pallet. It's either that or I grab my gear and carry it out on the prairie someplace. And I'll not be hearing argument, thank you."

"But . . ."

"What did I say? No argument, Dan, or you'll force me to walk away from some mighty pleasant hospitality."

"I just wish . . ."

"Hush, man. It's decided."

Hayward paused for a moment, then acquiesced with a nod. "However you prefer then."

"Before time to turn in, would you like to walk over to one of those saloons of yours so I can buy you a drink as a sort o' thank-you?"

"Oh, I appreciate that, Longarm, but I am not a drinking man." He grinned. "Not since I got married anyway."

"I understand that." In truth, Longarm did not see what one fact had to do with the other. A man just naturally enjoys a drink whether he is single or married. But then, he did not walk in Dan Hayward's boots.

Hayward stood. "It's about time for me to start showing the badge up and down the street."

"D'you want me to come along an' give you somebody at your back?" Longarm offered.

"Thanks, but that won't be necessary. This isn't a rowdy town, just a little high-spirited sometimes." His grin flashed again. "Besides, I've made that coach ride out from Toynbee. I know you're tired even if you don't want to admit it."

"Hell, Dan, I don't have any trouble admitting it.

Damn right I'm tired. Though I never have understood how sitting in a stagecoach wears you out so much worse than riding a horse for the same distance."

"Then let me tell Thelma that you will be the one on the pallet. She can go on to bed now, and I'll join her when I get done around three or thereabouts."

Longarm tossed away the stub of his smoke and followed Hayward inside the drab little shack the former cowboy was so proud of. First home of his own, Longarm guessed. First wife too. Apparently, Dan hadn't been exposed to the finer points of either.

Not that it was any of Longarm's business. No, sirree. He hung his hat and coat on pegs set in the wall and figured himself well set for the night.

"Hssst! Mr. Long. Are you awake?"

"I am now." He sat up. "What's wrong?"

Thelma Hayward was crouched beside his pallet holding a lighted candle. She was wearing a flannel nightdress and her hair was unpinned. It hung down in soft curls that reached halfway down her back. If anyone asked, Longarm would have to admit that the girl was mighty fine-looking. If anybody asked, that is.

"What's wrong?" he repeated, reaching for the gun belt that lay beside the bundle of laundry that served him as a pillow.

"Nothing is wrong," the girl said quickly. "I just . . . can I be honest with you?"

"Sure. Please do." He kind of hoped they could have this talk somewhere else, though. The way Thelma was leaning over him, he could not help but see down the top of her nightdress. Enough candlelight came through the cloth to put on display a pair of the biggest and most perfectly formed tits he had seen in quite a while. Big nipples too, and they were erect. For some reason, the girl was aroused. Longarm immediately got a hard-on.

She leaned even closer. Longarm forced himself to turn away, quite unnecessarily fumbling with the makeshift pillow as if plumping it up. Damn, but she was one fine-looking filly. "Could we move over t' the table?" he asked. "I'm, uh . . . I got a cramp."

"Where?"

"My leg."

"Which leg, Mr. Long?"

"This'un." He pointed toward his left calf.

"I can help."

What she did was of no help at all. Hell, she just made things worse. She leaned even lower, pushed his pants leg high, and began rubbing his calf as if kneading bread dough. If he had actually had a cramp, her touch would have been a boon. As it was, she only deepened his discomfort.

"That's good. Much better. Thanks." He pushed his pants leg down, stood, and stepped over to the table. She followed, so he pulled out a chair for her and seated the girl before he took the other chair for himself. "Thank you, Mrs. Hayward."

She set the candle over to one side of the table. She looked damned good in the soft candlelight. But then, she would have looked mighty fine in any light, he believed. "Call me Thelma. Please."

"I, uh . . . sure."

She smiled. "You are a very handsome man, Mr. Long. May I call you . . . what is it that Daniel calls you? Longarm?"

"That's my nickname."

"May I use it?"

"Of course."

"How did you come by that as a name?"

He shrugged.

She laughed. "I think I can guess. I think you are called that because you have a great big dick."

"Wha—"

"Oh, don't look so shocked. Surely you've heard the word before. And I can see how big you are. It shows right through your pants. You were looking down my dress, weren't you? Would it shock you to know that I wanted you to? Why else do you think I kept bending over like that? I have really nice tits, don't you think?"

"I, um . . ."

"Don't you think so?" She put the objects in question on display by pulling her dress open. They were magnificent. Firm. Pink. Perfect. Longarm thought he might squirt in his britches. And that was just from looking at them. Which he most certainly did. He couldn't *not* stare at the girl's tits.

"Feel them," she offered. "Take them in your hands and feel of them, why don't you."

"You know damn good an' well why I don't," he said.

"It's all right. Touch them. Would you like to lick them? Bite them? Would you like to play with my nipples?" She demonstrated what she was offering by rolling her right nipple between her thumb and middle finger. She giggled. "That feels so nice. It would feel even nicer if you did it."

"I . . . no, thank you."

"It is all right, Longarm. Daniel won't be back for hours."

"Girl, your husband not bein' here, him not knowin', don't have nothing t' do with it. You're a good-lookin' gal an' likely a fine piece of ass too, but I like Dan Hayward. He's a brother lawman. An' I won't repay that good man's hospitality by making him a cuckold. Thank you but no, thanks, Thelma."

"You don't know what you are missing," she said.

"No, an' I expect I never will. Now cover yourself, girl, an' go back t' bed."

"Are you sure? Last chance, mister."

"I'm sure. Now pull that dress together an' go back in there where you belong."

She pouted and sighed heavily, but after a moment she stood and closed the top of her nightdress. She stood there for a few seconds, then picked up her candle and retreated to the bedroom. Alone.

Longarm got up and found his coat so he could get a cheroot to take outside and smoke. He was so shaken by that encounter with Thelma Hayward that there was no point in trying to go back to sleep. At least his hard-on had subsided, thank goodness.

He lit his cigar and stepped out onto the porch, taking a chair with him. When he did, he came nose-to-nose with Hayward, who was standing in the deep shadow beside the door to his home.

"Evenin', Dan. Taking a break?"

"That's right. Just a short break."

Longarm had no idea if the constable had overheard his wife in there propositioning a guest in their home. And he damn well was not going to ask.

"Cigar?"

"No, I'm fine, thanks."

Longarm grunted softly. He set the chair down and settled onto it. Nice man, Dan Hayward. Longarm felt sorry for him.

Breakfast was hotcakes and fried antelope. Antelope was not Longarm's favorite meat due to the heavy flavor, but he could stand it. Likely, it was the most readily available game out here. There were some fine mule deer over on the mesas and some on the flats, but they too were tainted by the flavor of the sagebrush they routinely ate.

Thelma had reverted to her shy and quiet mode, acting ever so meek and solicitous, serving her husband first and their guest second. Only the men sat at the table while she flittered back and forth fetching more hotcakes, extra steaks, and refills on the coffee. The coffee again was exceptionally good.

"Your missus is a fine cook, Dan," Longarm said when he was full. He pushed his plate back and smiled. The comment was a lie, but not much of one.

"I'm glad you liked it. There's something I want to ask if you don't mind."

"Then ask."

"The thing is, I should be making myself available to help you while you are here, Longarm, but there are some things I need to do today. I don't mean to be rude, but I would like to beg off for today. Unless you need me to back you, that is. I can rearrange my schedule if I have to."

"Dan, I didn't come here t' get in your hair. You been more than kind, allowing me into your home an' all. No, you go ahead an' do what you got t' do. I'll get along just fine."

"Good. That, uh, that's good."

Longarm stood and stretched, thanked the constable's young wife for the meal, then got his hat and coat.

He stepped out onto the porch and paused there to set his hat more comfortably, and to reach into his coat for a cheroot and his vest for a match to light it with.

He had not yet stepped down off the Hayward porch when he heard a gunshot inside the shack, followed immediately by another.

Longarm whirled and leaped toward the door.

But he knew he was already too late.

Chapter 23

"Shit," Longarm mumbled. He shoved his Colt back into the leather angrily. Both of them were down, dammit.

Hayward had shot his wife square in the center of her forehead, then turned the pistol on his own temple. There was the smell of scorched meat heavy in the air along with the sharper aroma of burnt gunpowder.

There was another . . . Longarm inhaled deeply to sniff the air, then after a moment recognized the other smell as burned hair. Hayward's hair had been set briefly on fire by the powder charge behind the bullet that took his own life.

Thelma's dress was hiked up around her waist from the fall she took when she went under. She had good legs. Not soft and meaty the way so many big women have.

Longarm reached for another cheroot. "Reckon you heard what was said, eh, Constable?"

He wondered just who the hell he was supposed to

notify, Hayward himself being the one who should have been told about any other murder. Or suicide.

"Shit!" Longarm repeated as he turned and headed out the door to look for . . . He didn't know. The mayor, undertaker, some-damn-body.

The mayor turned out to be the blacksmith, a wiry individual named Cort Michaels. With the mine going strong, Michaels was buried in a backlog of jobs that needed doing. He was sweaty and grimy and out of sorts, and the news Longarm brought did nothing to improve his mood.

"You say Dan and his wife been murdered, mister?"

"Not exactly, though you could make a case that Thelma was murdered. Murder–suicide, I s'pose you'd call it."

"And you know this how?" Longarm noticed that His Honor the Mayor took a fresh and firmer grip on the hammer he happened to be holding.

"I know this because I was standing right outside the door. Thelma was cleaning up after breakfast and Dan was in there with her. Then I heard the shots. Went back in t' see what it was about, but o' course I already figured I knew. I'd've been glad to be wrong."

"And who would you be?"

Longarm smiled and said, "If you'll relax your hold on that hammer, friend, I'll reach inside my coat for my badge. I'm a deputy United States marshal workin' outa the Denver office o' U.S. Marshal William Vail."

"Vail, huh? I've heard the name."

Longarm nodded. "Billy is the one as signs all those wanted flyers you get in the mail from time to time."

"All right then. Let me see that badge. But bring it out slow if you don't mind."

"I don't mind at all, Mr. Mayor." In truth, Longarm could have put three bullets into Michaels before the man could finish drawing his hand back ready to strike, but there was no point in commenting on the fact. It would only sound like bragging, and Longarm wasn't much for brag or bluster.

He brought the wallet out and flipped it open to show his badge and let the mayor look it over. "That looks authentic enough," the man said.

"You're welcome t' send a wire to Billy if you like. He can confirm that I'm here on his authority."

"I don't think that will be necessary. You say Dan and Thelma are in the house?"

"Yes, sir. Them and a helluva lot of blood, so watch where you step. Both of them was head shots."

The mayor looked a little pale around the edges, but he did not comment.

"Is there anything you need me for, Mayor?"

"Not right now. I'll have to let Lou know. He's the town barber. Does all our burying too. We, uh, we'll probably hold the gathering late tomorrow morning and a coroner's inquest right after. We'll want you there for the inquest if you don't mind."

"I'll be there," Longarm promised. Such functions were not his favorite part of the job, but they were a duty that had to be performed.

"Thank you for . . . well . . . thank you," the mayor said awkwardly.

"Yes, sir." Longarm touched the brim of his Stetson and turned away.

He still had a job to do here, after all.

Chapter 24

Twin Rocks was a small town and news of every sort was likely to fly quick as bullets. News about the constable and his missus was probably all over the town by now and spreading fast. Along with it would be the juicy tidbit of a deputy U.S. marshal having been with the dead couple. That meant his anonymity would be gone in very short order. If he wanted to benefit from it, he would have to do it right away.

With that in mind, Longarm headed to the far edge of town where Adamson and Sons had their depot and corrals.

The company very likely was in critical need of the income they received from the Post Office. The corrals were in a poor state of repair. So were the sheds and the office that stood close by them. The lumber was cracked and warping, and what once had been a hitching rail beside the office building had become a pair of hitching posts when the rail had fallen down. No one had bothered to pick the rail up. It lay in the dirt, the rusty end of some nails sticking out where they could wind up in the hoof of any horse tied to one of the posts. Longarm was not overly impressed by the appearance of the Adamson outfit.

But then, appearances do not always tell the whole tale about anything.

Longarm stepped inside out of the bright glare of the sun. He immediately swept his hat off in deference to the young woman who was bent over a desk behind a rail that fenced off a customer waiting area holding two wooden benches and a water bucket with a dipper.

The girl looked up when she heard Longarm enter. She was probably in her early twenties. She had pale hair and delicate features. She began to speak, paused to cough into a handkerchief, then said, "If you are here for the outbound coach, you're several hours too early." She smiled and added, "I can sell you a ticket now, though."

"No, thanks. I, uh, I was hopin' t' speak with the owner."

"The owner of the line?"

"Yes, miss."

The girl swiveled her chair around to face Longarm and said, "May I ask what you wish with the owner?"

"Beggin' your pardon, miss, but that'd be between me an' him."

"Her," she said.

"What?"

"Her. The owner of Adamson and Sons is a lady."

"But . . ."

"I know. It is confusing. My name is Jessica Adamson, and I happen to be the owner of Adamson and Sons."

Longarm looked around as if he expected to see a man step forward to explain it all.

"My father was one of the Sons when the line was named. It was founded by *his* father. When he died, the ownership passed to me."

"Twin Rocks isn't that old, miss."

"Quite right. The line was founded in Kentucky. The family relocated here during the war." She did not bother specifying which war that would have been. But then, she did not need to. The War Between the States—or the War for Southern Independence as it was known by some—had been a watershed event that touched the lives of virtually every American.

"Sorry I interrupted you, Miss Adamson."

"You may call me Jessie. Or Jess as some do. Now, sir"—she smiled—"what is it that you wish to see me about?"

"I, uh, I was wonderin' how safe the mail is between here an' Toynbee. Long-term, I mean. I might be wantin' to mail some very valuable stuff, y'see. Once, twice a week."

"Then you should insure your parcels," she said. "Insurance is available for a modest fee."

"What about the safety o' the mail?"

"Sir, we have never had a loss due to theft."

"No trouble at all?"

"Not from theft."

"Anything else?"

"The only thing I can think of was once when an inebriated gentleman fell out and broke his neck. His widow claimed the fault was ours. She filed suit, but we won the case." She sighed. "Won the case, but were beggared by the lawyer's fees, damn him. It almost might have been better to pay what that passenger's widow wanted. I . . . I am sorry. I should not complain. All the more so to a stranger. Is there anything else you wish to know?"

"Yes, quite a few things," Longarm told her.

The girl pointed to the gate that gave access to the office portion of the depot. "Would you like to sit down and discuss your needs?"

"Yes, thanks." Longarm sat in the chair she indicated, crossed his legs, and placed the Stetson in his lap. "Tell me about the line," he said. "You say you've never been robbed an' when I came here yesterday, I noticed you didn't have no armed guard on the coach. Don't you use them?"

"We have never seen any need to hire a guard."

"Don't your mail contract require you t' have one for the protection o' the mails?"

"Not to my knowledge," Jessie Adamson said.

"You've never read it?"

She shook her head. "I never saw any reason to. Perhaps I should. Not that it really matters much."

"How's that?"

"You may not have heard, but there is a railroad line being built here from Toynbee. As soon as it reaches Twin Rocks, we can ask the Post Office to vacate our contract and pass it on to them."

"You want outa the mail contract?"

She nodded. "I already spoke with the district postal superintendent," she said. "We are obligated to continue service until or unless a substitute carrier is found. I tried to sell the line, but no one is interested in buying a stagecoach line that will be put out of business in a few months. I even tried to give it away, but nobody wanted it. If I were to simply abandon the line, I would be in breach of contract. The government would file suit and could even impose criminal charges against me. And frankly, sir, I have had quite enough of lawyers already." She made a sour face. "They are leeches. Human leeches."

All of a sudden, her hand flew to her mouth. "Oh, I . . . you are not a lawyer, are you? Oh, dear. I should have thought before I spoke."

Longarm threw his head back and roared with laughter. When he could speak again, he said, "No, Miss Adamson, I ain't a lawyer."

"Thank goodness. You, um, you do not work for the Post Office, do you?"

"Not that either, but I do work for the government." He took his badge out and showed it to her. "I'm a deputy marshal." He introduced himself.

"That is almost as bad." She sighed again. "I am not cut out for business. I have no head for it. No interest in it either, if the truth be known."

"What is it you figure t' do when the railroad gets here, Jessie?"

"As soon as I can get away from this mail contract, I intend to close the line. I shall sell the horses and the rolling stock. There is always a market for that sort of thing. Then I will be free to return to Kentucky. I have relatives there. And it is ever so much nicer than this dry, awful country. Kentucky is green and soft and beautiful. Have you ever been there?"

"Yes, I have."

"It really is beautiful, isn't it?"

"Yes, it is, Jessie. Very pretty." Longarm's opinion was that there was grandeur in the West also. But Jessica Adamson was not interested in hearing something like that. Not right now, he was sure.

After a moment, Longarm changed the direction of the conversation, saying, "I take it you have no objection to the railroad being built here then?"

"Oh, no. Quite the opposite. I am eager to see the first train arrive so I can get on with my life. Until then I am stuck here."

"So much for that theory," Longarm said.

"Are you referring to the troubles the railroad has had?"

"Yes, of course. How'd you know . . . ?"

"Oh, everyone knows about that. People shooting at the bridge builders. It is quite awful."

"But no one ever bothers your coaches?" he asked.

"No. Never."

"I sure wonder why that would be," Longarm mused aloud. "Why would anybody else care whether the town is served by a stagecoach as opposed t' a railroad?"

"I have no idea," Jessie said, "but if I learn of anything, I can promise I will tell you immediately."

Longarm stood. "Thank you, Jessie." He smiled. "Not that you've cleared anything up. Just made me more confused, not less."

He told her good-bye and stepped outside, hat in hand.

Chapter 25

Longarm had lunch in one of the town's saloons—at
least there were enough of those to go around—then sat
in on a card game in one saloon and rolled the bones in
another, mouth closed and ears wide open.

The talk was nearly all about Dan Hayward killing
his wife and himself. And about the fact that there was a
United States marshal in Twin Rocks. To investigate
Hayward, some said, claiming they had certain knowledge that that was the reason the marshal had come, to
arrest the Twin Rocks constable.

No one mentioned that Longarm was a deputy instead of the actual marshal. And one rather inebriated
gentleman who spoke with a Southern accent said the
stranger was not a U.S. marshal at all but a Texas
Ranger working in secret. The fellow sounded worried
when he said it, as if he spent much of his life looking
over his shoulder. Longarm took note of that one. When
he had a chance, he would mail the description to Austin
in case there were active warrants out on the gent. It was

a shot in the dark, though, and would not be worth the price of a telegram.

The result of all his casual conversation and quiet eavesdropping was that he had a fairly nice afternoon. He lost four dollars and a quarter at nickel-ante poker, but there were worse ways to spend time.

On the other hand, his time had produced no results. The townspeople were interested in the murder–suicide, not the railroad, and that was where their talk was focused.

Late in the waning day, Longarm stepped outside and glanced toward the western horizon. It was time to think about getting his things out of the Hayward shack.

By then too, pretty much everyone in town, including the mine employees who were streaming up out of the pit, knew who Longarm was. He was no longer anonymous, and any talk he overheard was very likely to be colored by that. He had long since noticed that people tend to speak more cautiously when they know there is a lawman nearby. Hell, he used to do the same thing before he first put on a badge. Caution is natural. And sensible. He understood that and felt no resentment because of it.

Supper was not going to be a problem as there were several cafés along the street where a man could get a meal, but the only two hotels were very crude affairs that were more barracks than hotels. For fifty cents a day, they offered two cheap and starchy meals and a room full of narrow board platforms where men could crowd in elbow-to-elbow and catch some sleep. With accommodations like that to look forward to, it was no wonder the saloons were so popular, Longarm thought.

He walked back to Dan Hayward's place, wanting to get his things out while there was still some daylight. The deeper pools of blood had congealed by now, but looked like they would still be tacky to the touch, and the place stank of blood and the shit both man and wife had expelled when they died.

Longarm had given some thought to the possibility of sleeping there while he was in Twin Rocks, but . . . he did not damn well think so. Not after getting a sniff of the residue of violent death. He moved around the blood as best he could to collect his gear, and carried it outside. He had no better place to put it, so he set it on the porch where only that morning he had enjoyed a smoke in Hayward's company. It likely would keep there.

His evening was equally unproductive, and he found no good solution to his housing problem, so eventually he went back to Hayward's to collect his things. He carried them around behind the shack and laid out a bed for himself in a rickety shed where Hayward had kept a long-unused saddle and a few decaying pieces of leather goods.

Before he slept, the image of Jessica Adamson kept coming into his mind.

Did she mean it about welcoming the railroad? Or was that only a false front put up to divert suspicion from herself?

He intended to find out.

Chapter 26

Funeral services for Dan and Thelma Hayward were held in the Adamson and Sons barn, which had been cleared out and cleaned up for the occasion. Longarm guessed the barn was the customary place for funerals in Twin Rocks because it was the only building large enough for a good funeral.

In this instance, size was not a factor. They could have held the entire proceeding in undertaker Lou Franken's barbershop.

The only mourners were the mayor, who seemed more worried about finding a replacement to serve as constable; Jessica Adamson, who seemed more interested in getting the use of her barn back; and half-a-dozen rough-looking men who did not bother removing their hats while Franken read a very brief passage from a small black book.

"All right now," Franken said when the two-minute service was over. "You boys back that wagon in so's we can load the coffins. You're taking both of them out to the JO for burying, are you, Joker?"

A tall man, who Longarm had taken to be one of the cowboys Hayward used to ride with, grunted. "I heard Dan was shot. Didn't hear that he done it hisself or I wouldn't've come in, Lou. This is costing me and the boys a full day's work. But I'm here now, and we got the graves dug this morning. I guess we'll take the son of a bitch and plant him for you. We'll take the slut too. Likely, nobody else would have her." It seemed no love had been lost between Joker Owens and Thelma Hayward.

"That's good of you, Joker." Longarm could not tell if the barber–undertaker was being sarcastic or not. If he was, the gibe seemed to pass right over the head of Joker Owens, the owner of the JO Ranch. "Will you and your boys be staying for the inquest?"

"Hell, no. We lost enough time already. I'll take the wagon back by myself." He turned to the men who were with him. "You boys can ride out wide and check the water holes this side of the big house before you come in. Coosie and me can pull these coffins off and dump them in the holes. Come in at the regular time. And don't worry. I ain't gonna dock your pay for only giving me half a day's work."

"Yes, sir, Mr. Owens. Thank you," one of the men said. He jerked his head toward the open wagon doors and led the cowhands outside.

Mayor Michaels said, "You need to wait until after the inquest, Joker. I can't release the bodies until the official inquest has been held."

"Fuck your inquest, Cort. If I don't start soon, I won't have time to get them in the ground before sup-

per. This has cost me enough already. If there's a problem, you know where to find me."

Longarm was surprised to hear Owens use rough
language in the presence of a lady, but he either did not
care, or possibly had forgotten, that Jessica Adamson
was standing only a few feet away.

"But . . ." Michaels began.

Owens was no longer paying attention to the mayor.
He went to the barn doors and supervised his men who
were bringing a buckboard inside, criticized the process
of loading the two coffins into it, then brusquely ordered
his men back to work when they were done. Longarm
did not think he would have wanted to ride for the JO
back when he was pushing cows around for a living.

As soon as his men were gone, Owens climbed onto
the seat of the buckboard and took up the lines. He
snapped his team into motion and drove out of the
stagecoach barn without bothering to say good-bye to
any of the locals. As far as Longarm could tell, Owens
had not looked in his direction once during the whole
affair.

Once the buckboard clattered out of sight, Mayor
Michaels turned to Longarm. "We can hold the inquest
now if you're ready."

Longarm looked around. "Without jurors or a coroner?"

"Lou here is our coroner too, and pretty much everybody in town is busy at this time of day. I think we can
waive the need for a jury to hear the evidence. For that
matter, you being the only witness, and you being an official representative of the U.S. government, I think we

can waive the necessity for testimony too." He cleared his throat. "You, uh, already told us what happened. Are you satisfied with that, Lou?"

"Yes, I am, Mayor. The wounds on those corpses is consistent with what this man said happened."

"So as coroner for Twin Rocks, Colorado, you can officially rule those deaths were by murder and by suicide, can you?"

"I so rule," the barber said in a solemn tone of voice.

Michaels shrugged. "I expect that would be it then." He turned to Longarm. "Do you have any questions? Any comments?"

"No, sir. I reckon if you're satisfied, so am I."

"Very well. If you would excuse us . . ." The barber and the blacksmith—the mayor and the coroner–undertaker—went off together, leaving only Longarm and Jessie Adamson in the barn.

"I'll help you get everything put back the way it was," Longarm offered.

"Thank you, sir."

Chapter 27

"Almost done," Jessie said a half hour later. "I just need to pitch some hay down."

"I'll help you."

"Thanks, but I can manage. There is hay from two different cuttings up there. You wouldn't know which I want to use." She smiled. "Just don't peep when I am on the ladder. I wouldn't want you to see my limbs."

"No. Of course not," Longarm lied. Like hell he wouldn't look at the girl's legs if he got the chance. Jessie wasn't a bad-looking girl.

He moved to the bottom of the ladder so he could support her if she lost her balance. And so he could more easily get a look at Miss Adamson's "limbs."

"Don't look now."

"Right."

She scampered three rungs up, then gave a high-pitched squeal of alarm as her left foot slipped and she toppled backward, falling completely off the ladder.

Longarm easily caught her, cradling her in his arms.

She weighed less than he expected actually. She felt warm and soft and really quite nice.

And her face was very close to his, practically nose-to-nose.

He kissed her lightly. Then again, this time more deeply. He could feel the girl's breathing quicken. Her chest heaved and she probed inside his mouth with her tongue. She tasted faintly of licorice, a flavor he remembered very fondly from when he was a boy.

After a moment, she drew back half an inch or so, but stayed close enough that he could feel her lips brush softly against his when she spoke. "There is a cot in the tack room."

"It's good t' be prepared." He kissed her again, then carried her to the tack room door. Jessie reached down and turned the knob so he could carry her inside the small room, which was cluttered with harness and odd bits of equipment. It smelled of neat's-foot oil and old leather.

But there was a narrow bed in one corner, probably kept there for use by a hostler.

Longarm set Jessica down on the side of the bed and sat beside her, his mouth locked on hers and his hands busy becoming acquainted with the curves and the textures of her. Her waist was smaller than he had thought and her tits larger. Her nipples were hard as pebbles.

"Do you like what you are finding?" she asked shortly.

"Mmm, nice."

Jessie pulled away from his embrace and reached up. Three quick motions and a shake of her head and her hair came tumbling down over her shoulders. She began unbuttoning her blouse.

Longarm stood to disrobe. When he stepped out of his balbriggans, he heard a sharp intake of breath. "Is somethin' wrong?"

"Lord, no," she said with an expression that was halfway between a grin and a leer. "It's just . . . you are so big." She reached out to touch him, running her fingertips up and down his shaft, peeling his foreskin back and examining the engorged head of his cock as if assessing the quality of a diamond. "Oh, my."

She very quickly shed her clothes and lay down on the cot, reaching up to welcome him to join her there.

Jessica Adamson was a very handsomely shaped filly. Her nipples were a dark red and her pubic hair a pale, curly blond. He could see her pulse flutter in the hollow of her throat.

Longarm pressed tight against her. He took his time, kissing her thoroughly. Kissing and then licking her throat. Her breasts. Running his hands over her belly and her thighs and then dipping his hand between her legs.

She was wet there, her juices wetting her hair and making it all the easier for him to find the tiny button of pleasure at the upper end of her vaginal slit.

He rubbed her clitoris gently while at the same time he sucked on a rock-hard nipple. After a few moments, Jessica's hips began to rise and pump in rhythm with his touch and her breathing became harsh and loud.

He could feel her flesh clench and pulsate.

She cried out aloud and thrust her hips violently upward in a spasm of pleasure.

"Oh, God, I didn't . . . I did not expect that," she said, her voice hoarse.

"But you didn't mind it, I hope," he teased.

"Can you do it again? Please?"

"Sure." He grinned. "But first I want t' dip the one-eyed snake in an' wiggle it around a mite."

Jessie shifted over to the middle of the narrow cot and pulled Longarm on top of her, opening herself to his entry, guiding him with her hand.

Her flesh was hot and slippery when it engulfed his cock. He lowered himself very slowly into her, giving her body time to adjust to his presence. And to his size.

She moaned and wrapped herself tight around him, clutching him to her with her legs and her arms, grabbing hold of the cheeks of his ass and drawing him even deeper inside her hot and willing body.

Jessica climaxed twice more under Longarm insistent stroking. And then he could feel the cum gather, ready for that sweet explosion of intense pleasure, and he loosed the reins, plunging wildly into her, hammering her body with his, pounding her belly and no doubt bruising her pussy.

She came yet again at the same moment that hot seed spat out of his cock to wash the inside of her pussy and spill out onto the scratchy woolen horse blanket that covered the old cot.

"Damn," she whispered happily when he finally was done.

Longarm could feel the insides of her thighs and the flat of her belly trembling in the aftermath of that succession of climaxes.

Apparently, it had been good for her. And mighty damn good for himself as well.

He thought she was drifting off to sleep, but after a

few minutes she opened her eyes and whispered, "Can we do it again?"

Longarm laughed. "You bet we can, lady. You just bet we can."

And he was right. They could.

Chapter 28

When they finally were dressed and standing on their own hind legs again, the sun had set and the last of the twilight was fading. Longarm nipped the twist off a cheroot and spat it onto the barn floor. He took out a match, but held onto it for the time being. It would have been rude to smoke inside another person's barn. Worse, it would have been dangerous. He could wait until he stepped outside.

"Where are you going now?" Jessica asked.

Longarm shrugged. "Gonna find something to eat, then prob'ly go back to Hayward's shed t' sleep tonight. I got no idea what I'll do in the meantime. Tomorrow morning, I figure t' go talk to some of those bridge-buildin' crews that've been shot at. Maybe I can figure this thing out."

"What if you don't? What will happen to the railroad in that case?"

"Lucky for me," Longarm said, "I ain't in the railroad construction business. I'll catch this jasper if I can. If I can't, then I expect it will be up to the railroad company t' hire a private army t' protect their people an' their property."

"Are you hungry?" Jessica asked, rather abruptly changing the subject.

He grinned. "After that good a fuck, yeah. A man is generally hungerfied after a hump that good."

"Did you say I was good?"

"Damn good, little lady. Take my word for it."

"Why, you big charmer, you." Jess laughed and rose onto tiptoes to kiss him. "Would you like me to make us some supper? We could, um . . . you could sleep at my place afterward."

Longarm put an arm around her and squeezed. "I got nothin' better t' do this evenin'."

She jabbed an elbow into his ribs. Longarm yelped and doubled over. "If you can't show any more enthusiasm than that, I just may take back my offer," Jessica said.

Instead of speaking, he grabbed her and yanked her close, then wobbled her knees with a kiss that threatened to suck her tongue clean out of her mouth.

"You do," she said, "have a way with words. Come along then. But don't pay any attention to the mess. I wasn't expecting company."

Women. Why the hell do they always fret about appearances? Longarm silently mused.

They sure can be useful, though.

"I don't keep any meat in the house," Jess explained as she tied an apron around her waist. "It always spoils before I get around to cooking it. And I never have company in. Do you want me to get Mr. Simon to come open his shop so I can get you some meat?"

"Got any potatoes?"

"Yes."

"An' some lard?"

"Of course."

"Then fry me up a big mess of taters, Jess. I've sure et worse than that. Set down here an' I'll help you peel them."

"You don't mind doing women's work?" she asked.

"Honey, I don't carry no woman along t' do my cooking when I'm on the trail. Cooking ain't exactly woman's work anyhow. It's just something that's necessary. Sit down now an' fetch them taters out."

"What will you do now? Where will you go?"

He helped himself to a seat at the table and said, "I ain't for certain sure. I'll likely hire a horse so's I can ride out. Talk to some of the construction crews. Look around a little maybe. I'll just have t' play it by ear, as they say."

Longarm took out his pocketknife. Jessica took one look at the stains left by years of hoof-trimming and handed him a proper kitchen knife to use instead. Then she got down a large bowl and a poke of only slightly wrinkled potatoes. She sat down beside him at her tiny kitchen table and the two bent to their task of peeling and slicing the spuds.

"What's your theory about the problems the railroad is having?" Longarm asked while they worked.

"I don't really have one," she said.

"You haven't heard any whispers?"

"Not about that exactly."

"What then?"

Jessica finished peeling a potato and deftly sliced it into the bowl. She picked up another and started carefully peeling it, her brow wrinkled with concentration as she tried to take off only skin. Longarm, on the other hand, flashed his knife rapidly, not caring how deep under the skin he cut.

"I don't really know anything," she said after a moment. He had begun to think she was ignoring his question.

"But you've heard what?"

"Some are saying the railroad will not be completed."

"Because of the sabotage at the bridges?"

"Maybe. I don't know."

"Who is saying this?"

She looked up from her careful peeling. "I don't know. Everyone. No one. Just . . . people."

"That would be as good for you as the completion of the line, wouldn't it? I mean, if the railroad comes through, you can pass the mail contract to them. If the railroad abandons their effort, your stagecoach line will have some value again and you can sell it if you wish. Either way, you can go back t' Kentucky like you plan."

"I hadn't thought about that." She hesitated, lost in thought for a moment. When she looked at him again, she smiled. "You are right. I win either way, don't I. Things are in limbo now, but I will be all right in the long run whatever happens." Her smile became wide and her eyes sparkled. "Thank you for pointing that out to me." She laughed. "I can think of several ways I may be able to thank you. Later." She toyed with the buttons at the neck of her blouse and winked at him.

"Peel faster," he said.

Chapter 29

The only livery in town was a sideline to the stagecoach business. It too was operated by Jessica. Sort of.

"I don't get two calls a year for the hire of a saddle horse," she told him in the morning while he was shaving. "I have those old saddles in the tack room . . . you saw them yesterday."

"Uh-huh." He pulled at the side of his face to smooth the skin and prompt the whiskers to stand out where they could be sliced away, hopefully without taking any flesh along with the wire-hard whiskers. He wanted to get rid of them. Jess had begun complaining about them by morning. In fairness, he supposed they did hurt.

"The only animal I have that I know is saddle-broken," she went on, "is that spotted mule in the corral. He has a nasty disposition and I should have gotten rid of him a long time ago, but he is as tough as an old boot. I've never known him to play out. You can use him if you like."

Longarm shifted over to the other side and again dragged the razor lightly over his skin, then flipped the excess saving soap into the basin of warm water and attacked the rather delicate job of shaving his chin. "I'll take him. The government will pay whatever your day rate is."

"Oh, Custis, I couldn't charge you for him."

"The hell you couldn't, pretty girl. I'll be on official business, and you're entitled to be paid. Damn!"

"What?"

"I nicked myself, that's what." He wet a fingertip and dabbed at the thin trickle of blood that was welling up in the cut.

Jessica giggled. "Is that why you wear that mustache."

He turned away from the mirror and grinned. "It might could be one of the reasons."

"All right. I shall accept the government's money for the use of my mule."

"That's damn decent of you. Now hush yourself while I finish this part, will you?"

Jessica cooked breakfast for the two of them, then walked with Longarm to the barn. He carried his own saddle along rather than risk the cinches on a piece of junk like those in the tack room.

The brown mule was a big sonuvabitch. "He looks like a cross between a moose an' a giraffe," Longarm said as he led the mule out of the corral to the barn, where he'd dropped his saddle. He set about saddling the critter.

Jess sighed. "I've never seen a giraffe. Or much of anything else. Have you?"

"Ayuh. I've seen a giraffe. Seen the elephant too, but that's something else again."

"What do you mean?"

He smiled and stepped into the saddle. "It's an expression. I'll explain it later."

"Will you be back tonight?"

"Dunno. I'll be back when I get here. Not a minute before." He leaned down and planted a kiss on her that again left her knees weak. The mule chose that moment to bog its head and buck, and for a moment there Longarm thought the beast was going to unseat him.

He touched the brim of his hat as a safe form of good-bye—he didn't want to spook the mule again—and got the hell out of there. Obviously, the mule needed to have some of the sass ridden out of it.

There were two rifles trained on him as he rode into the work crew's camp, and a third man stood, legs spread and arms crossed, waiting for the stranger to reach them. Off a hundred yards or so in three of the four principal directions, he could see men standing guard, watching out across the prairie. The one who had been on duty on the west side of the camp walked behind the mule, a Henry rifle cradled in his arms and suspicion plain in his expression.

It was a six-man camp and four of them were standing guard, Longarm noted. That left only two men in camp to do the actual work. No wonder the railroad was not making much progress. He wondered if the bosses knew the men were giving their first priority to staying alive. Which was sensible, but not very damn productive.

"Howdy." Longarm took out his wallet and displayed his badge before he said anything else. These fellows looked like they expected to be jumped by a swarm of savages at any moment. "I'm Deputy United States

Marshal Custis Long, an' I hear you boys been having a little trouble from time t' time. I come out here hopin' you could tell me more about it."

"Thank God someone is paying attention," said a stocky fellow with a spade beard and eyeglasses. "Step down, friend. We'll tell you everything we know, little though it be."

"Thanks."

Longarm stepped down from the mule, and the guard who had followed him in took the animal's reins. "There's a patch of good grass over here. I can picket him on it."

"Fine, but don't let him get loose. I'd hate like hell to have t' walk back." Longarm paused and added, "An' be careful about those teeth too. I haven't seen him try an' kick anything, but he's tried a couple times to take my toes off. I think the ornery sonuvabitch would scalp you quicker'n an Injun could."

"Ben, bring out a cup and pour the marshal some coffee. This might take some time," the bearded man said.

Chapter 30

By the third camp he visited, Longarm was so full of coffee that he sloshed when he walked. If he had been that full of information, he would not have minded, but the only thing he'd learned was that the construction gangs were frightened so bad they could hardly get anything done. And just from observing, he was not sure that what they did accomplish was done correctly. Their culverts looked like they would collapse the first time an engine drove over them.

He ate lunch at the third camp—a solid feed of mule deer that had been browsing in the sage flats and tasted like it—and headed east toward the last of them.

"Just follow along beside the wagon road," the foreman at the third camp told him. "You can't miss it." He shook his head angrily. "I sure wisht we could catch up with these bastards, though. Quick as we get a roadbed laid out and a bridge built, we go on to the next gully or wash that needs to be crossed. The next time we come back by, our bridge has been burned. Damn things go up like matchsticks if you pour enough coal oil on them. We build the sons of bitches; they burn 'em down."

"And you've never seen who does it?"

"No, sir. Never caught a glimpse of 'em. But we know it's people working for that damned stagecoach outfit. Oh, we try and catch them at it. But if we post a guard, nothing happens. If we leave be, they come in and burn our trestles. We even put up scarecrows, sort of. We made us some dummies to put up like they was standing guard. The miserable sons of bitches, excuse my French, burned the fucking scarecrows." The fellow shook his head. "It's getting us down, and that is the natural truth. We thought about retaliating. You know. Grabbing the coaches when they go by and burning them. But we was told not to do that or we'd surely find ourselves locked up, those stagecoach people being locals who have the vote here. If you know what I mean."

"You're sure it's them, though," Longarm said.

"Yep. It has to be."

It occurred to Longarm that that opinion had been expressed before. By Bertram Hancock back in Billy Vail's office. There was no doubt in Hancock's mind, or in the minds of his men, that Jessica Adamson was responsible for the arson.

And they were dead wrong.

He wondered exactly where they had gotten the notion, but when he asked, it was always that someone said, someone thought, someone believed. No one actually *knew.*

A little misdirection? Longarm wondered. Sort of like the sleight-of-hand artist who gets his mark looking over *here* while he really is slipping that card out of *there.*

A jasper who was good with his hands and clever with his line of bullshit could make a good living by fooling the rubes fresh out from under mama's apron.

Of course, that same fellow could get a knife in his gut if he tried to fleece the wrong gent.

Longarm thought mayhap he should wander over to Toynbee and see if anyone in the railroad office there had any idea how this rumor about Adamson and Sons being behind the sabotage had gotten started.

Hell, he was already halfway there. Why not let Jessica's iron-muscled mule take him the rest of the way.

He thanked his hosts at the construction camp and stepped back onto the mule, twisting his boot away at the last moment to avoid those powerful yellow teeth that snapped in his direction.

"Good day, gentlemen. Thanks for the grub."

"Any time, Marshal. We'll always be glad to see you here."

Longarm was about four miles farther down the line when he saw a plume of dark smoke rise from behind a low hillock. He saw the smoke and heard the distinctive report of a gunshot.

"Shit!" he muttered aloud as he put spurs to the mule.

Chapter 31

The smoke was getting thicker. Something was burning fiercely over there, and he had a pretty good idea it was another one of the bridges.

That did not make sense. So far the saboteurs had only burned bridges that were completed and from which the work crews had moved on. No one had been hurt by this other than the railroad shareholders, and they had not been physically harmed. Longarm hoped like hell that trend had not suddenly changed.

He topped the hill. At the bottom, he could see a blazing latticework of heavy timbers and the tents, tools, and other gear of the fourth construction crew.

He could see . . . shit! He could see what looked like bodies scattered in and around the camp.

He could see . . . a flicker of bright light close beside a pile of timbers and a puff of white smoke.

Gunshot!

Longarm knew it was already too late to duck, but human nature made him do it anyway. He leaned down close to the mule's neck at virtually the same moment a heavy slug slammed into the animal's forehead.

The back of the mule's head exploded, covering Longarm in a spray of blood and brain and bone, and the animal pitched forward on its nose.

Longarm was off balance from trying to duck, and could not get any purchase with his feet or knees to propel himself clear of the falling mile. He went down with it, face-first into the ground.

He more heard than felt the impact and then . . . then he felt nothing. Nothing at all.

He came to slowly, becoming reattached to the world one small bit at a time. He smelled dirt. Felt the scrape and tickle of grass stems. Very carefully worked out the fact that he was lying facedown on the ground. An ant was crawling down the side of his nose, and was close to wandering into his nostril. The little sonuvabitch was not welcome there.

Longarm brushed it aside, and in doing so discovered that his left arm and hand worked.

He pushed with his right arm and levered himself into a sitting position.

He was dizzy and more than a little disoriented. It actually took him several moments to work out what was wrong with his right leg and why he could not get up. His right boot was trapped beneath the body of the dead mule.

The memory came back. The smoke. The burning camp. The bodies. The gunshot. And now . . .

He braced his left boot against the seat of his saddle and pushed, then again harder, while at the same time trying to pull his right leg free. It took a while, but he managed it. Jess wasn't going to be most happy about her mule, he thought. That, however, was not the worst of his worries. It wasn't even close.

After two abortive attempts, he got to his feet, swaying drunkenly at first. His Stetson lay in the grass a dozen feet away. He retrieved it, and in putting it on encountered dirt and pieces of grass stems on his face and in his mustache. He brushed his face off, combed out the mustache as best he could using his fingers, and gave his clothes a thorough brushing with the flat of his hand. He felt gritty and dizzy and sick to his stomach.

But he was by God alive and on his own hind legs.

He picked up his Winchester—the saddle would have to stay where it was until he could get some help because there was no way he was going to shift the deadweight of that mule, not by himself there wasn't—and began picking his way very cautiously down the slope toward the camp below.

Chapter 32

There were four of them. All dead, shot at close range. Footprints and the position of the bodies suggested that someone had come into the camp, forced the men to line up, and then shot them.

There were four bodies, and on the ground close to their campfire were eight brass cartridge casings. Longarm picked up one. The cartridge was a .32-20, not exactly rare but certainly not common either. He slipped the brass case into his pocket.

He also looked inside the tent where the dead crew members had lived. There were four cots and bedrolls, so this was not a matter of one of their own going loco or flying off the handle as the result of an argument. The dead men constituted the entire work crew that had been at this camp.

"Shit," Longarm grumbled aloud.

There was little he could do here, though. He was trying to work out if at this point he was closer to Twin Rocks or to Toynbee, because with Jessie's mule dead it looked like he would have to walk back. Then he heard a low rumble, and looked up to see a high-walled freight wagon coming down the opposite slope. The outfit was pulled by four scruffy and unkempt-looking cobs.

The wagon followed the stagecoach road into the wash these dead men had been trying to bridge, then turned toward the camp.

"Hey!" the driver shouted when he belatedly realized what had happened here. "Who are you, mister? What happened to these fellas?"

Longarm showed his badge. "There has been murder done here, friend, and I've been set afoot. I need your help."

"Sure, Marshal. What d'you need me to do?"

"Climb down off your rig. You can help me get my saddle off that mule laying up yonder. Then I'll need the borrow of one o' those horses of yours."

"Say now, I don't know as I can let you do that," the freighter protested.

Longarm smiled at him. Sort of. The expression held no warmth in it whatsoever. "Trust me," he said. "Yes, you can."

The speckled brown horse was trained to drive, not ride, but it was a patient and agreeable old piece of shit. Longarm felt like an idiot sitting atop it, and he could not get it to go faster than a slow, plodding walk no matter what he did with his spurs or other goad. There was no such thing as neck-reining either. He had to saw back and forth at the reins to convince the beast to change direction, and the animal's back was so wide he felt like he was sitting on a table instead of a horse.

But it went in the direction he demanded and it was as steady as a town-square statue.

There was scant sign left in the sod around the construction camp, but he found some hoofprints in the wash that was being bridged, and was able to work out that the shooters had approached the camp from the south, riding down inside the wash where they could not be seen from ground level.

There were two horses, therefore two men. Either both of them favored the .32-20—mighty unlikely, he believed—or only one of them did the shooting.

Not that that really mattered. Both the sons of bitches would hang when he caught up with them.

Sabotage of a railroad was one thing, but all that was involved there was the destruction of property. Murder upped the ante.

Longarm's reading of the sign suggested the two sneaked up to the camp, forced the bridge builders onto their knees, and then shot them down like cur dogs. Then they set fire to the timbers of the nearly finished bridge. They seemed to have been in the process of dousing the leftover timbers with coal oil when Longarm's arrival interrupted their fun.

He tried to remember, but he had no recall of seeing a second shooter in the camp when he came over the crest of that hill. He could barely remember the movement of one person. That was the one who shot at him. The others . . . he brought the mental picture back to mind and examined it as closely as he was able. As best he could recall, there was one living person and only one. The other figures in his mental image—he carefully tried to work out the position where they lay—were those of the dead crewmen. And the one shooter.

He had no memory of seeing a second living person in the camp. But then the other man, the one who had not done the shooting, could have been down in the wash with the horses or inside the tent. Just because Longarm did not remember seeing him did not mean there was not a second man. And there definitely had been a second horse.

It was that second horse that helped Longarm work out the trail. It had big feet and it was fairly clumsy, dragging the toe of its off hind foot every two or three steps. The scrape marks it left behind were faint, but from the back of that slow and heavy draft horse, Longarm had plenty of time to work out those marks.

And he was in no hurry. He figured he was on this trail for as long as it took.

Chapter 33

The ranch house was a low, rambling affair made of sawn timbers but with a central core of adobe brick. Longarm guessed it was an outfit that had started small and grown over the years, expanding here at the headquarters as it expanded out on the range as well.

He had no idea whose place it was, but the trail he was following had brought him here, coming up to the ranch buildings from behind.

On the east side, he could see the beaten tracks of a road that passed beneath a crossbar. A steer skull with horns as wide as a wagon is long dangled from the middle of the beam, and there probably was a brand on or above it, but Longarm could not see that from the back of the place.

He rode around to the central yard and dismounted. A man wearing a greasy apron and carrying a dish towel in his hands stepped out of the nearest building. "Nobody invited you to step down from that horse, mister."

"That's right," Longarm agreed. "Nobody did."

The cook scowled. "You best crawl back on that ugly

thing before I beat shit out of you and load you on him."
He took a step forward and balled his hands into fists.

"Friend, I ain't in the mood to take sass. I'm here on
official business, an' if you try an' lay hands on me, I'll
put a .45 slug square in the middle of your fat gut."

The cook still looked belligerent. But he took that
step back again so he was standing in the doorway of
his cookshack. Likely, that was where he felt most comfortable. And in charge of things. "What, uh, official
business you say you're here on? What sort of business
would that be?"

Longarm showed his badge. "I'm a deputy United
States marshal, and I'll have your ass breaking rocks at
Fort Leavenworth if it pleases me t' do so."

"Just asking," the cook quickly said.

"Now you know."

"Yes, sir. Now I know."

"I followed some tracks here," Longarm said. "I
want t' know who rode in here a little while ago."

"Marshal, we got people coming and going all the
time, and that's the truth. Besides which, I just don't pay
no never mind to who's where or what everybody is up
to. I got my work to do and that's all I know about."

"Who would know?"

"The *segundo* would, I suppose, but he's off taking a
delivery of range beef to the Ute Reservation. Or, of
course, the old man."

"Who would that be?"

"Mr. Owens. Joker, he's called by."

"Owens? This is the JO spread?"

"Yes, sir. Marshal. You didn't know that?"

Longarm shook his head. "I came down from over

174

yonder way. I didn't know. I met Mr. Owens at the burying for Dan Hayward, though. He seemed like a man as is set in his ways."

"You could say that. I've known a lot worse bosses, though. He feeds his people good and pays regular as clockwork. Truth is, I've known a lot worse men than Mr. Owens too. I've never known him to lie. If Mr. Owens tells you something, you can take it to the bank."

"Then I expect he's the man I need to talk to."

"You'll find him in the house."

"Good enough." Longarm led the brown cob to a nearby water trough and let him have a drink, then tied him to a corral rail. There were two horses standing inside the pen. Both of them showed sweat on their hides. The sweat was still wet even though in the dry heat of the west slope any liquid tends to evaporate quickly.

Longarm slipped inside the corral and felt of the animals to make sure. When he climbed out, he noticed there was only one saddle hanging on the rails. One saddle, two blankets, and a pack frame. He turned back to the cookhouse. "Excuse me."

The cook returned to his position at the door.

"Are you feeding any line camps?"

"Not at this time of year, Marshal."

"Roundup crew?"

The cook shook his head. "They already made the gather for the delivery I told you about. They won't be branding and earmarking until fall after the blowfly season is past."

"That's what I thought. How d'you haul your supplies from town?"

"Got a wagon, Marshal, just like everybody else."

"All right, thanks."

Longarm left the cook to his stove and took a quick sashay around behind the buildings at the JO headquarters.

By the time he was done, he was frowning.

He thought he had figured out "what." But he had no idea about the "why" of it.

His stride lengthened as he headed for the house.

Chapter 34

"Oh. It's you. What do you want?" the owner of the JO said when he came to the door.

"I'm Dep—"

"I know who you are, dammit. I saw you just yesterday at the fucking funeral, didn't I? Now what do you want, I asked you."

"I want to come inside and talk with you," Longarm said.

"Not today. I'm going over my monthly accounts. I don't want to be bothered with no company."

"I'm afraid I'll have to insist," Longarm told him.

"Fuck you." Owens took half a step back and started to slam the door shut in Longarm's face. Longarm was a little bit quicker. He inserted his boot between the door and the jamb.

"Damn you!" Owens barked.

"Damn you," Longarm snapped back at him. "That hurt."

"Get out. This is my home. You have to have a warrant to come in here uninvited. I don't see a warrant."

"If I may quote you, Mr. Owens, 'Fuck you,'" Longarm shot back at him. "I am in what you call close pursuit. I am pursuing and intend to apprehend a murderer."

"Not in here you aren't. There's no one in this house but me."

"Now, sir," Longarm said with a thinning of his lips that might have been mistaken for a smile, "that right there is exactly the thing I was gonna ask you. I need t' know who-all is on the place right now."

"Fine. Now you know. It's me and Coosie, nobody else. Now get the fuck out of here."

"Joker Owens, I am placing you under arrest for the mur—"

The tall ranch owner snatched a lamp off a table beside the door and threw it at Longarm's face.

Longarm ducked and the lamp smashed into a thousand pieces, scattering broken glass and coal oil all over the front porch of the ranch house.

Joker Owens disappeared inside, again trying to slam the door shut when he did so.

Longarm recovered and stepped inside. The interior of the house was dark, and it took a moment for Longarm's eyes to adjust. By then, Owens was gone.

Longarm had seen rabbit warrens that were laid out with more of a sense of order than this house was. Each wall seemed to be built of a different material. Each floor in each room differed as well. Or so it seemed on first impression.

The place was a maze of heavy furniture and dark colors. The walls were hung with saddles and spurs, moth-eaten serapes and saddle blankets.

And guns. There were rifles, shotguns, and revolvers hanging on pegs in the front room and God knows where else in the place. Hell, there were even native bows and arrows and a collection of swords and polished steel helmets that looked like they dated back to the days of the ancient Spanish conquistadors. Longarm figured he could pretty safely conclude that Joker Owens was armed now.

He stopped for a moment and listened, then walked softly down one of several halls that extended away from the entry foyer, glancing inside each room as he came to it. Parlor, office, bedroom, dining room, kitchen, another bedroom, another. It was a big house for only one man, and surely had not been built for one man alone. Yet every indication—the décor, the weapons, the mess left here, there, and everywhere— said only one man occupied it. There was no woman's hand visible here, and likely there had not been for many years.

Longarm came to the back of the place, turned around, and started going through the house again, more carefully this time. He was almost back to the foyer when he heard the faint creak of a hinge that had not been oiled quite recently enough.

He spun, Colt in hand, dropping into a low crouch as he did so.

The blade of a sword swooshed through the air close enough to clip the top of his hat and send his Stetson flying.

The good thing was that it was the hat and not his head that was knocked off, because that sword stroke was intended to behead him.

Longarm instinctively came back upright, his legs acting as powerful pistons to drive his shoulder into Owens's midsection.

He heard a loud huff of air as the breath was driven out of Owens. Longarm followed the shoulder with the back of his wrist, bringing it and the barrel of his Colt up into Owens's balls.

Owens cried out and fell back. He lost his grip on the sword. It went clattering across the flagstone floor.

Longarm stood upright and backed a few steps away.

Owens was down on his back. It was obvious that he was hurting. It was equally plain that he was enraged beyond reason. Though Longarm was standing there in front of him and he himself was writhing on the floor in agony, he nonetheless tried to draw down on Deputy Marshal Long.

Longarm shot the son of a bitch.

Chapter 35

"You've killed me, damn you."

Longarm kicked Owens's pistol out of reach, plucked a foot-long dagger out of a sheath at the man's waist, and tossed that aside too. Then, but only then, he took a look at the rancher.

Owens had a neat, round, red hole just below the sternum. It bubbled wetly, the bloody froth rising and falling with Owens's attempts to breathe. "You're in bad shape, Owens."

"Is there time to bring a preacher out from Toynbee?"

"I doubt it," Longarm said. "You'll be dead long before anybody could get in t' town, find a preacher man, an' get back out here again."

"Damn you," the rancher wheezed.

"You shot those men, Owens. How's come you did that?"

"Damn railroad. Cut my range in two. Cattle won't cross railroad tracks. Damn rails would take grass away from me. Right-of-way would be deeded to the railroad. Bunch of stinking sodbusters'd come out. Tear up the ground. Ruin everything I've built here." Blood began to flow more freely from the hole in the man's belly, trickling down his side and soaking into the shirt that Longarm had pulled open.

"Cows have no problem crossing railroad tracks," Longarm said.

"Even so. Take my grass away. Couldn't . . ." He stiffened as a bolt of pain struck him; then he went limp again. "Couldn't let that happen."

"I can kinda understand you burning those culverts an' bridges," Longarm said, "but why'd you murder those men?"

"Didn't . . . didn't mean to. Thought they left that coulee. Went in to burn the damn bridge. They saw me. Recognized me. I had to put them down or they . . . they would've told. Didn't have much choice. But how . . . oh, shit, this hurts . . . how'd you find me? How'd you know?"

"Coal oil," Longarm said. "I found those empty coal oil tins out behind your tack shed and found the panniers with some spilled coal oil soaked into the canvas. And like you said, it's only you and your cook here on the place. It had t' be you as pulled the trigger on those men."

"I regret . . . regret shooting them. That was a mean thing. I hate to go out with such a thing on my head."

"The sky pilots say if you ask, you can be forgiven."

"I've done some low things." The blood was as much pink as it was red now. It was watery and full of bubbles. "Are you . . . are you sure I'm dying?"

"Yeah. I'm sure."

"Shit," Joker Owens said.

It was the last word he ever spoke. The man closed his eyes, shuddered violently for a moment, and then expired. It almost seemed that he deflated, as if the substance went out of him along with his spirit.

"Shit," Longarm repeated in a whisper.

Then he stood, his knee joints creaking, and picked up his hat before going out to find the cook. Somebody had to be told that the boss was dead. After that, it was no longer Longarm's worry.

GIANT-SIZED ADVENTURE FROM AVENGING ANGEL LONGARM.

LONGARM AND THE OUTLAW EMPRESS
0-515-14235-2

WHEN DEPUTY U.S. MARSHAL CUSTIS LONG STOPS A STAGECOACH ROBBERY, HE TRACKS THE BANDITS TO A TOWN CALLED ZAMORA. A HAVEN FOR THE LAWLESS, IT'S RULED BY ONE OF THE MOST POWERFUL, BRILLIANT, AND BEAUTIFUL WOMEN IN THE WEST...A WOMAN WHOM LONGARM WILL HAVE TO FACE, UP CLOSE AND PERSONAL.

AVAILABLE WHEREVER BOOKS ARE SOLD OR AT PENGUIN.COM

Explore the exciting Old West with one of the men who made it wild!

**AVAILABLE WHEREVER BOOKS ARE SOLD OR AT
PENGUIN.COM**